Praise for Lex Valentine

A Reviewer Top Pick at Night Owl Romance - "Shifting Winds is a HOT read that will make you turn on your air conditioning and look for your significant other."

5 Angels from Fallen Angel Reviews - "Lex Valentine put so much more feeling into this book, and I loved every minute of it... If you are looking for an erotic paranormal romance story that is emotionally and sexually charged, then I highly recommend *Hot Water* to be added to your reading list."

4 Brainys from Cerebral Reviews - "The emotions in Hot Water wrung me out - in a good way - and the touching scenes, thoughts, and actions in this book will linger for some time to come."

Rated 5+ Stars by Jessewave – "Lex Valentine is a gifted writer as she creates a world for her dragons that is so real I could taste and feel it. Her writing is engaging, vibrant and fresh and her characters are incredibly three dimensional and larger than life."

5 Kisses by Talking Two Lips Reviews - "I love the emotion and draw this novel has... When these two men get together there is such chemistry I think my fingers were scorched reading this one!"

Rated 4.5 by Book Wenches - "This is a very well-written and sensual tale that will have its readers believing in fate and dragons and love as they are completely enveloped in Ms. Valentine's Darkworld."

The Tales of the Darkworld Series by Lex Valentine

Book 1: Shifting Winds
Book 2: Hot Water
Book 1 and 2 printed in Tales of the Darkworld Volume 1
Book 3: Fire Season

Pink Petal Books

Pink Petal Books, an imprint of Jupiter Gardens Press, publishes romance novels where the relationship is primary. It doesn't matter if you want to read super erotic or sweet inspirational books. Pink Petal Books believes that love is a beautiful thing, no matter what form it takes. For more information about Pink Petal Books visit http://www.pinkpetalbooks.com/.

Additional Titles by the Author
Tales of the Darkworld Book 1: Shifting Winds
Tales of the Darkworld Book 2: Hot Water

The scanning, uploading and distribution of this book via the Internet or via any other means without the permission of the publisher is illegal and punishable by law. Please purchase only authorized editions and do not participate in or encourage the electronic piracy of copyrighted materials. Your support of the author's rights is appreciated. Permission is granted to make ONE backup copy for archival purposes.

This is a work of fiction. Names, characters, places, and incidents are either the product of the author's imagination or are used fictitiously. Any resemblance to actual events, places, organizations, or persons, living or dead, is entirely coincidental.

TALES OF THE DARKWORLD BOOK 3: FIRE SEASON

ALL RIGHTS RESERVED

Copyright © Lex Valentine, 2009
Cover Art ® 2009 by RottNRoll Productions

Edited by Mary K. Wilson
ISBN# 9780982543573

Electronic Publication Date: July 2009
Print Publication Date: October 2009

This book may not be reproduced or used in whole or in part by any means existing without written permission from the publisher, Jupiter Gardens Press, Jupiter Gardens, LLC., PO Box 191, Grimes, IA 50111

For more information to learn to more about this, or any other author's work, please visit http://www.pinkpetalbooks.com/

Fire Season

Lex Valentine

*To Kathy,
I'm so glad you love my guys as much as I do. Love, Lex*

PPB

Dedication

To the phenoms Jason Edding and Ethan Day for beta reading my first M/M novel. And to Maurya because no one does "Open, open, open" better.

Author's Note:

The Tales books don't go in order chronologically. Each story can stand alone, but read together provide the reader with a comprehensive view of the Antaeus family and their friends and connections. The series spans ten books and in each book there are characters the reader will recognize from prior books. Here's a mini-time line of the chronological order of events for the books that have been in the series thus far.

Fire Season, Shifting Winds, Hot Water, Shifting Winds epilogue

Prologue

Alfred Stone leaned back in the sauna, casually adjusting a white towel over his naked lap. His voice sounded as casual as his demeanor, but to his one man audience, the tone rang more warning bells than a three alarm fire.

"I am Magia. My job is to ensure that nature's intended matings actually occur."

Sean Antaeus stared at his best friend in shock. "You have got to be joking." Nothing in his life had prepared him for the words Alfred had spoken. It wasn't so much what Alfred had said about Sean's younger brother, it was what Alfred had revealed about himself.

The Darkworld held people with power and powerful people. Sean had been living in a dream world thinking that Alfred, as the head of the Funeral Directors Guild, was merely a powerful person. Now, he knew the truth.

"Sean, I wouldn't have told you if I didn't think you could handle the information. My job isn't always easy. Your family has been especially hard. In fact, I need Marius' help too. His family is going be just as tough." Alfred's brow crinkled with worry as he spoke.

Sean arched a sardonic brow at him. "So you're letting Marius in on the secret too?"

A sigh escaped Alfred.

Sean thought it sounded rather dramatic and long suffering, which made him feel like he'd walked into some kind of set up.

"If you knew what I was up against, you wouldn't ask me that," Alfred replied in a morose voice.

Now, Sean knew he'd been played. Maybe not a lot, because at the core of it all, he knew instinctively that Alfred had spoken the truth, but Sean also could tell when he'd been manipulated. After all, he was a master of manipulation himself. *Took one to know one.*

"So you're telling me that both Diandra and I were the victims of your...gift?" Sean put his friend on the spot.

Alfred shifted uncomfortably on the sauna's seat. "Not victims, Sean. Recipients of a power that managed to keep you from fucking up your life. If it weren't for me, do you think either you or your sister would have ended up mated? Both of you were so stubborn and arrogant, refusing to see the truth, not wanting to be seen as weak."

Alfred made a rude sound and his gaze locked with Sean's. "If I hadn't butted in and used my gift to help you, both you and Diandra would be single today and unhappier than you could ever imagine," he said solemnly.

Sean bit back his own sigh. He couldn't imagine. His life would be awful if he didn't have his mate and wife, Careen. Yet, getting to the place where he'd accepted that he had a mate, a woman he loved beyond everything else in his life, had been a particularly rough road. The same had held true for his sister Diandra. Her path to love and marriage had been every bit as rocky. Now, Alfred made it seem like neither he nor Diandra would have managed to mate without a nudge from Alfred's power.

"Please tell me that you didn't pick our mates," he growled, feeling unnerved by everything Alfred had told him.

"Of course not. Those are nature chosen. But it's my job to ensure that those who are resistant become...more amenable to having a mate." Alfred smiled, something Sean knew he rarely did. "I smooth the path in any way I can without disrupting the natural flow of a mating."

Sean's brain raced as he absorbed Alfred's words. "And now you're telling me that Holden is in trouble?"

Alfred nodded solemnly. "A lot more trouble than you and Diandra put together. I need your help, Sean, or your brother will be unhappy until the day he passes to the Afterlife."

"Fuck." Alfred had him. Sean loved his younger siblings fiercely. He would fight anything that threatened their lives and happiness.

"So you're in." Alfred looked at him expectantly, triumph already shining in his eyes.

This time Sean did sigh. "Yeah. I'm in."

He shook hands with Alfred and realized that he'd sealed a pact of duplicity and manipulation as he did so. Luckily, being Machiavellian was second nature to Sean, and he bet Alfred knew that fact quite well.

Chapter One

The first to arrive, Holden slipped into his seat and opened his leather covered notepad with irritation. He disliked rah rah meetings. Despite all the team building pep talks, things always went back to the way they had always been...with his oldest brother Sean wielding his iron fist and micro-managing while he and his other brother Declan struggled not to let Sean overwhelm them.

In Holden's opinion, corporate life had been worse while Declan had been gone. During Declan's tenure at a European conglomerate, Sean had refused to replace him. Instead, Holden's oldest brother had taken on acquisitions himself in his brother's absence. Sean had gone crazy buying up whatever he could. Declan had a lot more finesse and savvy when it came to choosing the funeral homes and cemeteries that offered the best value. The company needed Declan's firm hand and cool head when it came to acquiring new businesses and Holden had been relieved when his brother returned to Antaeus International.

Declan's return to the company heralded the end of their sister Eden's term of employment in the corporate world. Her contributions to the company were myriad, but all of them had been tainted by her unhappiness in that environment and Sean's determination to keep her there. It had all come to a head not long after Declan's return. Eden had ditched her marketing job at Antaeus International, packed up her cameras, and headed to New York City. Within a few months, she'd become the fashion industry's new hot photographer, making her name shooting nearly naked men in designer underwear. Sean's fury knew no bounds over her defection and both Holden and Declan had borne the brunt of it.

The door opened and a muscular man with unruly black curls entered the room. Holden cocked one brow up at Vahid Delrey, his brother Sean's right hand man and the company's Chief Operating Officer. Vahid had also been Eden's live-in boyfriend for two years prior to her departure from all things Antaeus. Holden had always been amazed that Vahid had retained his cool demeanor, his deepest emotions, if he had any, masked from everyone when Eden had dumped him. Not for the first time, Holden wondered how Vahid had ever gotten together with his free-spirited sister. They seemed like such polar opposites.

"This is another attempt at a team building meeting, isn't it?" Holden asked as Vahid took the chair opposite him.

A dry chuckle escaped Vahid. "You know Sean. He may suck at something, but his determination won't let him stop trying to master it anyway."

Holden felt his lips curl in a derisive smile. "My brother is a force unto himself that's for sure."

Now, Vahid's brows rose. "Nice way of saying he's an arrogant ass."

The door whooshed open and the subject of their conversation strode in with Declan and another man behind him. Holden's nose twitched. The scent of spearmint assailed him.

"Thanks for the compliment, Vahid," Sean said smoothly, a sardonic expression on his hawkish features.

Declan took the chair at the foot of the table, seating himself on Holden's left. Sean took the chair at the head of the table. The spearmint scent intensified as a man Holden didn't know took the seat beside Vahid. More staff rushed in to join the meeting, but Holden found his gaze caught by the newcomer. Intense green eyes gazed back him, an indefinable emotion churning within them. Holden had no clue as to the man's identity, but an odd sense of familiarity pricked his awareness as he stared into those enigmatic eyes. It was as if knew the man, but couldn't place where or how.

The green gaze shifted as a tall, blonde woman strode into the room. Dressed in an unrelenting black suit and matching silk shirt, her pale hair twisted into a neat chignon, Emily Carrington looked like a fashion model until one noticed her stern visage. As one of the most powerful people at Antaeus International, she held the company's purse strings in her long-fingered, capable hands. The new man smiled at her as she took a seat beside him. Her expression turned smug and the new guy's identity dawned on Holden. The wunderkind of the death care industry's financial sector, Garret Renquist.

Sean and Emily had somehow managed to lure Garret from his position as the head of finance for Stone Mortuary Services, a job he hadn't even held very long. Alfred Stone had hired him away from the biggest British mortuary conglomerate in the hope of turning him loose on the Funeral Director's Guild's financials, a big project that Alfred had spearheaded as the head of the FDG. Instead, Sean and Emily had whisked the whiz kid to Antaeus International. With an internal smirk, Holden briefly imagined the acquisition of the stock market genius taking place over a round of golf. His brother Sean golfed regularly with Alfred and Marius Granville of Granville Cemetery, the oldest cemetery in their part of the Darkworld. Holden figured the three powerful men brokered all kinds of industry related deals during those golf games. Something told him that Garret Renquist might just have been one of those deals.

"Let's get started," Sean said from the head of the table. "This will be a short meeting anyway since we're all leaving."

"Leaving?" Holden asked, startled. What the hell was his brother up to now?

Sean's intense golden stare turned on Holden. "Yes. Leaving. I'll get to that in a minute."

Holden watched as his older brother's hawk-like gaze settled on the new guy. "Has everyone met Garret? Garret Renquist is our new Chief Investment Officer. He'll also be working in the capacity of Budget Director under Emily, which means he'll be working with all of you on your budgets. He comes highly recommended and has a great reputation for increasing a company's investment returns. If you haven't had an opportunity to introduce yourself to him, I suggest you do so over the next four days..."

Sean's voice trailed away and Holden mentally braced himself. He knew that tone. Sean was up to something that would probably irritate the hell out of him. His brother's suggestion that everyone introduce themselves to Garret was a thinly veiled order. Since Eden's departure, Sean regularly did things that he knew would force his younger brother out of his comfort zone and push the limits of his patience. In the past, Holden had always bounced back from Sean's Machiavellian power trips. Lately, he found himself beyond angry when his brother's machinations involved him.

Turning his gaze to his notepad so his brothers wouldn't see the anger beginning to simmer inside him, his nostrils flared as the scent of spearmint wafted toward him again. Who the hell smelled like mouthwash?

"I'll be closing this meeting in a few minutes, but we will reconvene tonight at six over dinner at the Gargoyle Resort. You are all to go home and pack. We're headed out to the mountains for a retreat."

Holden's head shot up and his eyes met his older brother's. A gleam of triumph lit Sean's amber eyes. Holden's jaw tightened. Sean had made his feelings clear a few weeks before regarding the woman Holden had been dating. Since Sean had never interfered in his sex life before, Holden had been surprised that he'd even mentioned her. He'd brushed off his older brother at the time. Holden really didn't give a shit whether Sean liked who he was fucking. It was none of Sean's business and it wasn't serious anyway.

Now, however, Sean's machinations had pissed him off and cost him money. Holden had cleared his calendar for two days so he could have a long four day weekend. His intent had been to spend those days in a sexual stupor at an exclusive spa in Santa Barbara. The steep deposit he'd put down with his reservations for two would now be lost, and the woman he was seeing would require placating. Fury rose within him. The loss of the money didn't irritate him so much, but the thought of having to soothe Gina's ruffled feathers made Holden furious with his oldest brother. Even though Gina had a tongue that could lick all day, she also had a rather bitchy attitude that showed up when she didn't get her way. Thanks to Sean, Holden would now be the recipient of the bitching rather than the licking.

"This will be an opportunity for us to work on some team building and strategizing. It will also give you all a chance to spend some time with Garret to see how he can help each of your departments maximize your budgets."

Sean's smile widened as Vahid got up and handed out brochures and packets to everyone. Holden opened his folder and stiffened. Sean had paired everyone up, forcing them to share rooms. Sean and Declan were together. Vahid shared with Todd Ryan, the Chief Technology Officer and Holden's draw was...the new guy. His head shot up and his gaze collided with Garret's intense stare. A little smile quirked up one corner of the man's mouth. That little smile kicked Holden's irritation up a notch. He frowned, wondering what it would take to get Vahid to trade with him.

Holden's eyes tracked Vahid around the table. When the head of Operations returned to his seat, he cocked a brow up at Holden. His smirky expression dashed Holden's hopes for a trade. Vahid obviously knew that Sean had put the new executive with his youngest brother for a reason.

Fuck! Anger tore through Holden at his brother's little games. Grinding his teeth together, he eyed the itinerary included in the packet. All the rah rah stuff was there and, even worse, there were scheduled strategizing sessions between each set of partners. Great, now he had to talk business with the finance geek all weekend instead of spending his time getting blown and fucked by the hottest woman he'd dated in a year.

The law degree and MBA hanging on his office wall had made Holden the company's General Consul and Chief Legal Officer. He dealt mostly with contracts and the mergers that Declan arranged. Anything related to litigation got shuffled off to a firm on retainer. Holden answered directly to Sean, but spent most of his time working with Declan. Looking at the itinerary for the next four days he couldn't believe Sean hadn't paired him with Declan. It made better sense to him because he and Declan were in the middle of some delicate takeover negotiations with an Australian company. He didn't have any strategizing to do with the bean counter, Holden thought with annoyance. Pairing him with the whiz kid had to be yet another Sean Antaeus production.

Holden watched Sean close the meeting. An odd glow of triumph lurked in the golden depths of Sean's eyes. Holden's dragon senses pinged. A triumphant Sean wasn't necessarily a good thing for the members of his family. He jerked his attention from his brother and gathered up his things, fury propelling him out of the board room. Fuck Sean. Maybe he'd just not show up at the retreat. That would teach his brother.

The scent of spearmint caused his nostrils to flare. He turned his head to find that Garret Renquist had followed him out of the board room. His frown deepened.

"I gather you're unhappy about being paired with me."

Visions of a cool woodland waterfall flitted through Holden's mind at the sound of the British accented baritone. Holden didn't know why it hadn't dawned on him that Garret was British. The man had come from a British based company.

Holden stepped into his office and Garret followed. Holden shut the door and waved the financial whiz kid toward a chair. As he sat down behind his desk he noticed that Garret's green eyes flickered over the wall of certificates, awards, and degrees. For a moment, Holden again had the sense that he knew the man. The spearmint scent apparently came from Garret. Holden's office smelled like a bottle of mouthwash.

"You're the General Consul." Garret's clipped British accent made the words sound almost accusatory, though Holden knew that wasn't his intent.

With a nod, he gestured toward the wall of plaques. "I went to Harvard Law School. I wasn't top of my class, but close." He smiled a little and joked, "All the Boston beauties kept me from studying too hard so I missed out on the top three spots."

Garret's eyes glowed a little and his mouth quirked up in the same smile he'd displayed in the board room. "I've been to Boston. There are a lot of good looking women there. It's a very academic town, isn't it?"

Holden nodded absently. Something about the spearmint scent bothered him, but like the sense of familiarity he had when he looked in Garret's eyes, he couldn't quite place it. He studied the man before him more closely. They had similar builds and were about the same height. Garret stood perhaps an inch taller and he appeared to be a little leaner than Holden. His chestnut brown hair was cropped close around the back of his neck but fell over his forehead with a wave in front. He had a boyishly handsome face, but his reserved demeanor made him look rather stern. Holden wondered if the golden boy of the stock market ever had any fun. He certainly looked all business.

With a mental shrug, Holden studied the man's very green eyes. They held an open expression, but Holden felt sure that behind that expression, Garret Renquist was quite guarded. Had he been the new guy, he'd be totally on his guard.

"I'm not unhappy about being paired with you. I'm unhappy about the whole weekend," he explained, reaching out to grasp his pen, twirling it absently in his fingers. "For one, my brother Sean likes to play at being the puppet master, making us all dance on strings. For another, I had plans."

Two beats of silence followed his words. Then Garret's eyes clouded, the emerald green irises darkening. Holden figured the man didn't like the idea of Sean being a manipulator. It sure as heck wasn't something he'd want to know about his boss's boss on the first day of a new job. He felt a little sorry for Garret now. He'd obviously had no idea what Sean Antaeus was like when he accepted the position at Antaeus International.

"Look, we'll just have to make the best of it, as we do with any of these team building things Sean springs on us. I'm sure we'll find something to work on during the strategy sessions," he said easily, hoping he hadn't scared off the new guy. Sean would kill him if he did.

One of Garret's brown brows arched up. "You don't think we're a good match?"

Holden blinked at the man's odd choice of words. "There's not a lot of interaction between my department and yours. I work more closely with my brother Declan. Declan works with Emily. I'm not sure why Sean put us together."

Garret's mouth quirked knowingly as if he had knowledge Holden didn't. Resisting the urge to shift uncomfortably in his chair, Holden snuck a glance at the guy. He sat there cool as a cucumber, his expression enigmatic, while Holden could barely keep from fidgeting.

Holden looked down at his hands then and dropped the pen he'd been twirling. When he raised his head, his gaze collided with Garret's. The scent of spearmint intensified and a nervous sweat broke out on the skin between Holden's shoulder blades, making his clan mark itch. He sucked in a breath as realization hit him.

"You're a dragon."

Garret nodded, the enigmatic expression giving way to amusement. "Your natural enemy. I'm a green."

Holden made a rude sound. "The dragon clans haven't fought in a millennia. And even then, there was nothing natural about it. All the wars were about power. Not color or clan. Legend says we were all one color in the beginning. Our natural enemies were humans, not each other."

A huge smile broke out on Garret's face. "You're a purist."

Holden's stomach lurched. Geez, the man had the most brilliant smile he'd ever seen. He shook his head. "I'm a realist. Dragons were not born to kill each other. We were never each other's natural enemies. Humans on the other hand instinctively want to be rid of any being stronger than themselves. Their fear drives them."

Both of Garret's brows rose, but his smile stayed intact. "A psychology major."

"Biological Anthropology." Holden grinned, beginning to relax. Maybe the weekend wouldn't be so bad after all. In fact, it would be perfect if he had a victim. "Hey! Do you play...?"

"Tennis," Garret finished for him with a nod toward Holden's college trophies. "Although not in your league."

"That was years ago. My reflexes aren't so fast anymore. I sit at a desk all day after all."

Garret's brow cocked up again. "You don't look so out of shape."

Holden shrugged. "I'm not, but I don't play much anymore and to stay at the top of your form you have to play every day. I had the skill to go pro, but not the drive. I like working for my family." He grimaced. "My brother is a pain in the ass, but I wouldn't work for any other company."

"Your brothers, this company...Antaeus is a powerful name in this industry," Garret said quietly. "I was flattered that Alfred wanted me for the FDG and Stone. I was floored when Sean said he'd pay me more to come here."

Holden laughed. "I'll bet Alfred was tweaked. He's one of Sean's closest friends so I'm sure he gave my brother an earful, but the rest of us would never know it."

"Strangely, Alfred took it all very calmly, as if he had expected it to happen."

Holden prepared himself for the sense of familiarity when he met Garrett's gaze. "I'm sorry if I gave you the impression I was pissed at having to share a room with you."

Something indefinable flickered in Garret's eyes. He rose from his chair. "It's all right. I've been feeling a bit out of my element today so I overreacted." He turned toward the door. "I'll see you up at the resort. Maybe we can get in a couple of rounds of tennis while we're there."

Holden smiled. "I'd like that. Welcome to Antaeus International, Garret."

The other man looked back over his shoulder. "Thank you." A brief smile flashed across his face and then he was gone.

Holden sat staring at the closed door for long minutes, the scent of spearmint lingering faintly in the office. The anger he'd felt at Sean's manipulations had fizzled during his conversation with Garret. He should know better than to get pissed anyway. It never changed anything. Holden had never known anyone to get his way more than Sean.

On his way to the elevator, he ran into Declan. "Nothing from Australia?" he asked.

His brother shook his head. "Not yet."

They both stepped into the elevator. As the door closed, Holden said, "Why did Sean stick me with the new guy?"

Declan shrugged. "Why does Sean do anything? Everything is about control with him."

"Has he messed with your private life too?" Holden's gaze sharpened as he looked at his older brother.

"What private life?" The words were cool and sardonic with a bitter edge.

Sympathy washed over Holden. His older brother had a huge thing for Elysia Granville, one of the most powerful women in their industry. However, she was engaged to the industry's biggest asshole, Austin Stone. Holden didn't understand how such a smart woman had ended up with such a monumental jackass. A woman like her belonged with a man like his brother, not a weasel like Austin.

"I gather Sean's little jaunt to the mountains is interfering with your plans," Declan said, his voice rumbling out of his broad chest.

Holden looked up to find his brother's expression filled with understanding. "Yeah. It's gonna cost me a bundle too between the deposit on the suite at the spa and keeping Gina from being disappointed."

Declan's eyes twinkled. "Buy her an expensive bracelet. She's mercenary enough to be placated by rocks."

The elevator stopped at the underground garage and they headed toward their assigned parking spots. "Why do you and Sean think that's all Gina wants from me?" Holden grumbled as he watched his brother's tall form move toward his Mercedes.

Declan shot him an amused glance over the roof of the car. "Because it's obvious?"

Holden grimaced. "Money isn't the only thing she wants. She likes my cock too."

His brother grinned, white teeth flashing in his tanned face. "Well, she should. Especially when the man attached to the cock buys expensive presents. Just watch it with her, little brother. She wants the gold ring with rocks and you just want to get your rocks off."

Holden walked over to his SUV. "Yeah, well, she can want the ring, but that doesn't mean she'll get it. I'm not the marrying type."

"Neither was Sean." Declan laughed and unlocked his car, the headlights flashing as the alarm disarmed. "I'll see you at the resort. Good luck appeasing Gina."

As Holden drove to his condo, he pondered his brother's words. He knew Gina wanted to marry him. He knew she was dazzled by his job, his money, and his good looks. He also knew that a woman like her would never fit in his family. For all their money, the Antaeus siblings were all about home and hearth and true mates. Holden wouldn't dream of marrying a social climber like Gina. A woman like her could never be his mate. Maybe Sean's interference wasn't such an inconvenience after all. Although left with only his hand to see to his sexual satisfaction, being rid of Gina and her demands was more of a relief than he'd wanted to admit.

Holden's condo was in a high rise condominium complex only two blocks from the beach. He drove into the underground garage and parked in the space reserved for the penthouse. His footsteps echoed in the cement structure as he walked to the elevator. Thoughts echoed in his head too. Everything from Declan's bitterness to Sean's manipulations to the prospect of kicking Garret's ass at tennis. The weekend was starting to look up.

In the elevator, he punched in the security code that took him to the penthouse level. The elevator opened onto a foyer that had but one door, his. Unlocking the penthouse door and automatically disarming the alarm, Holden stepped into his home. From his living room, he had an unparalleled view of the coast in both directions. His expensive, but comfortable furniture softened the starkly modern architecture. It was a bachelor's home, not meant for entertaining in spite of its size.

Holden jerked off his tie and jacket, tossing them on the brown leather couch. In the kitchen, he pulled open one side of the huge brushed aluminum refrigerator and took out a bottle of water. As he drank, he eyed the crayon drawings stuck to the refrigerator with magnets. His sister Diandra's twins were the only Antaeus offspring. He, Declan, and Eden were unmated. Sean and Careen hadn't had any children yet. Holden figured his brother wouldn't have kids until all his siblings were mated. It was a very Sean way to go about things.

For himself, he didn't even wonder if he had a mate. He didn't particularly care. Kids and a white picket fence and the kind of woman who would want that life were so not his style. On the other hand, society type women and career women weren't really his type either. People with that kind of driven personality irritated him which is why he was no longer pissed at missing his weekend with Gina. He really only had one use for her and now that he realized it, he was too nice a guy to continue fucking her when he didn't even like her.

As he headed for his bedroom, Holden wondered if Garret Renquist was the driven type. He didn't seem that way, but it was tough to tell with wonder boys. Things seemed to come so easily to them that if they were driven, those around them never noticed. Holden opened his packed suitcase and changed some of the items so that now his clothing was more suited to a mountain business retreat rather than a beachside spa. Once the suitcase was ready to go, Holden picked up the phone and called the exclusive jeweler his family always used. He ordered an elegant ruby bracelet to be delivered to Gina that evening and headed down to his car.

He figured he'd call Gina while he drove so she'd know he wasn't lying to her about having to go to the mountains. It was going to be an uncomfortable call, so doing it while driving also gave him the excuse of the call dropping if he got tired of listening to her rage or whine. The more he thought about how unpleasant the call would probably be, the more he just wanted to be rid of her. And so, when he was halfway up the mountain pass on the way to Gargoyle Resort, Holden found himself breaking up with Gina over the phone.

She whined. She raged. She cursed him in Italian. And then he hit a dead spot and the call dropped. Sighing with relief, he shut off his cell phone. The remainder of the drive to the resort relaxed him and by the time he arrived, Holden looked forward to playing tennis with Garret. He loved tennis and rarely got the opportunity to play anymore. He hoped Garret played well enough to challenge him.

Holden's shared suite turned out to have two bedrooms and a well stocked wet bar in the sitting room between the two rooms. Since he was the first one there, he picked one of the rooms and unpacked. As he stowed away his suitcase, he heard the door open. He walked into the sitting room to find Garret standing in front of the door, taking in his surroundings.

"It's a two bedroom suite," Holden said with a grin. He gestured toward the door across from him. "That one's yours."

Garret returned his smile and picked up his suitcase. "Thanks."

"Can I get you a drink while you unpack? It's an hour until dinner and there's a fully stocked bar here. No mini bottles." Holden's nose twitched as the spearmint scent reached him. He'd never smelled cologne like that before.

"That would be great. Just a glass of red wine if they have it, please," Garret replied as he walked toward his room.

Holden heard the sound of Garret opening his suitcase and then the closet door. He searched through the wet bar's stock of alcohol looking for wine and found a full size bottle of Merlot and one of Cabernet Sauvignon. The Merlot was a decent vintage and he decided he'd have a glass. He pulled out a corkscrew, expertly removed the cork, and poured two glasses before ambling over to Garret's bedroom door.

The British man had his back to Holden, putting folded shirts in the dresser. Holden noticed absently that they were dressed similarly in khaki slacks and polo shirts. Without the suit jacket covering his torso, it was obvious that Garret was taller, yet leaner, with a narrow waist and broad shoulders.

"Here's your wine. They had a decent vintage of Merlot. Surprised me," Holden said as he watched Garret finish unpacking. The whiz kid had an elegance of movement that was graceful in its economy. Certainly not what he expected of a bean counter.

Garret stowed his suitcase, turned, and took the glass of wine from Holden, their fingers brushing briefly. A frisson of awareness trickled down Holden's spine at the touch of Garret's warm hand. Something about him affected Holden physically. First, there was that odd prickling of his clan mark that he'd felt earlier and now the touch of their hands made him feel flushed. Not to mention that damned spearmint scent that assailed his nose.

Magia. The thought flashed through Holden's mind and he wondered if Garret was more than just a green dragon. Sometimes dragons had magical abilities, but usually those that did belonged to the community of Magia rather than the dragons. He wished he understood what unsettled him so much about the other man.

Abruptly, he turned and walked back into the sitting room, opening the slider to the balcony. He stepped outside into the crisp mountain air and sat down on a comfortable patio chair. Garret followed him and took the chair on the other side of the small table.

"This is a very tolerable Merlot."

The smooth British accent caused Holden's clan mark to prickle yet again and even though they were outside, the spearmint scent was just as strong as it had been inside. Holden didn't understand why the man had such an odd impact on him. Again, he wondered whether Garret was

Magia. It would certainly explain his reactions to the guy. His annoyance at being unable to figure out Garret rose.

"So how are you settling in?" he asked abruptly. "Are you looking for a place to live?"

Garret nodded, his eyes twinkling a little as if he had a secret. "Yes. Something with a view of the coastline, rather more modern than not. Nothing I need to spend time keeping up...that sort of place," he replied.

"You should look around my neighborhood. There are lots of very nice condo complexes like that. In fact, I can ask my association manager for a list of availabilities if you'd like." Holden couldn't believe what had just come out of his mouth. He didn't need the new guy living in the same building! Not that he could take the words back now...

"Thank you. I would appreciate that very much."

Garret's cool, even tones set Holden's back teeth to grinding silently, although for the life of him, he didn't know why. "I'll call her this weekend and have her fax a list to you at the office," he muttered, lifting his wine glass to his mouth and gulping down half the contents.

The emerald eyes of his companion glittered knowingly. Frustrated by how the man unsettled him, Holden knocked back the rest of his wine and rose to his feet. "It's almost time for dinner. I'm going down to the restaurant."

Garret's expression turned sympathetic as if he knew how Holden felt. He didn't speak, but those uncanny eyes watched him like a hawk. A muffled sound of exasperation escaped Holden. "I don't get you," he ground out in a low tone that expressed his frustration. "Are you Magia or what? Cause I'm all edgy and weird around you and I don't know why. My clan mark is prickling. You smell like a pack of spearmint gum. Every time I look at you, I think I know you from somewhere, but I can't place where! What the hell is going on?"

The glow in Garret's eyes intensified as he rose to his feet, facing Holden. "Think about what you just said to me, Holden," he said quietly. "Think about what those things might signify. I'm not Magia, but as far as you're concerned, I'm something far more rare and important."

He walked over to the sliding door and then stopped, looking back at Holden. "Open your mind, Holden Antaeus. Life doesn't always fit in neat little boxes or compartments. Things happen for a reason."

Garret stepped into the sitting room, disappearing behind the blinds. Holden stared at the empty doorway for long moments. Emotions tugged inside him. Even though Garret had gone inside, Holden could still smell his spearmint scent. His eyes narrowed thoughtfully. That scent...his dragon lore came rushing back to him and his jaw went slack with shock.

Holy shit! No fucking way!

He shook with reaction, his fingers clutching the empty wine glass convulsively. It couldn't be true. It wasn't possible. Somehow Sean had set him up. His brothers were punking him, playing him off against the British man somehow. The guy was probably some tennis stud who would kick his ass six ways from Sunday the moment they took their rackets out. Yet, how could they have manufactured his scent and Holden's reaction to that scent?

Holden stormed into the suite, fumbling a little with the door and the blinds. As he stumbled into the sitting room, Garret turned, his hand dropping from the handle of the suite's door. Their eyes met, Garret's sympathetic. Holden knew his expression was wild with disbelief. This couldn't be happening!

Garret sighed loudly and turned his back on the door, facing Holden fully. "It's not as complicated as you think, Holden," he said quietly. "I don't know why either. I just know it *is* and I recognized you right away. What you do with the knowledge, how you deal with it, is up to you, but you cannot change it unless one of us dies."

A growl began deep in Holden's chest as fear took hold of him. "Something's wrong!" he burst out, his emotions wildly overwrought.

Garret shook his head. "No. Something's very right." He moved, crossing the room swiftly to stop a few inches from Holden who wanted to recoil but somehow managed not to. His voice when he spoke was soft, but firm. "Holden, you're my mate."

Chapter Two

The disbelief on Holden's face filled Garret with apprehension.

"But I'm not gay!"

Garret flinched at Holden's words. He'd known it wouldn't be easy to convince the black dragon that they were mates. Lord knew it had hit him like a ton of bricks as he'd sat in the conference room, Holden's crisp lime scent taking hold of his senses. In fact, the scent had tipped him off to what had happened. No one had ever had such a clear cut scent to him before. And it was obvious that no one else had noticed. As Holden stared at his brother and then down at his folder, Garret had had a few moments to study him.

Holden Antaeus seemed familiar to him and for a few moments he figured it was because he looked so much like his brothers, whom Garret had already met. But as he stared at the ink black hair, the tanned skin, and lean aesthetic features with the unmistakable Antaeus stamp upon them, he realized the familiarity had nothing to do with Sean and Declan and everything to do with Holden himself. He felt drawn to the man, something inside him tugging and pulling at his emotions. The knowledge of what Holden meant to him slipped into his consciousness quietly. As Garret gazed at the youngest Antaeus brother, he knew he saw his destiny.

Sean's announcement hadn't been met with pleasure by any of the executive staff seated at the conference table except for Vahid Delrey, the COO. Garret had already pegged him as Sean's right hand and had it confirmed when the man got up to hand out the retreat packets. The anger he'd felt coming off of Holden struck him square in the chest. That's when he'd realized convincing the man that they were mates would be the biggest battle of his life. Lawyers liked to wheel and deal and argue. A man like Holden, secure in who, and what, he was, wouldn't be easily convinced to switch sides because his mate was a man and not a woman. Of course, maybe the man was also bisexual. That would certainly help, but his gut told him that Holden Antaeus was as straight as a ruler.

Deciding to face the whole situation head on, he'd followed Holden to his office. Looking at the "wall of fame" the man had made Garret realize his mate's pride. Intelligent. Athletic. And...nice. Right away Holden had let him know that he wasn't angry with him, but with his brother. A nice man. A fair man. One who didn't believe in the old dragon tales, but instead held a clear vision of equality between the dragon clans. He was a man Garret could be proud to call mate. If he could get Holden to accept him as such.

Now, standing eye to eye, a few inches separating their bodies, Holden completely unnerved and freaked out, fear crept into Garret's veins. He had to convince Holden of the truth. Somehow, they had to work things out.

"Neither am I," he said quietly, trying to keep his voice steady and calm.

Holden's golden eyes flared with emotion and Garret could see him holding onto his composure by a thread. "If I'm not gay and you're not gay, why the fuck are we mates?" Holden growled.

One step forward. Holden hadn't refuted the evidence of scent, recognition, and the awareness of a growing emotional bond. However, having a man for a mate confused him. Something Garret totally understood.

"I'm bisexual, Holden," he explained.

Holden shook his head dazedly. "It still makes no sense, Garret. I'm not gay. I'm not bi. I'm not into men at all. I never have been." His face hardened. "I'm a pussy licker not a cocksucker!"

Garret flinched again. *One step back.* He resisted the urge to grab Holden by the shoulders and shake him. The sense of fairness and equality he'd gotten from Holden earlier in the day was completely missing now. The man's mind wasn't open to the possibilities at all.

"Mates aren't just about sex. They're about compatibility and happiness. Whatever force creates these matches does so in order to bring about the happiness of the people involved." Garret felt like a professor outlining basic dragon biology and theology. "It's not gender specific but person—dragon—specific."

Holden's nostrils flared and a trickle of smoke emerged, giving away his emotional turmoil. "So the fact that we're supposed to recognize each other, mate, and have sex together for the rest of our lives has nothing to do with the fact that we are both men and one of us isn't interested in sex with men?" he asked in an acid tone.

A leaden sensation began to take hold in Garret's chest. This wasn't going well at all. Like Holden, he didn't understand why they were mates, but at least he was open to the possibilities. He knew the consequences of not mating once you'd found your mate. He'd once heard them detailed by someone who had watched another be slowly driven insane by the pain. If Holden never came to accept that they were mates, their future was bleak.

Garret turned away toward the door. "I don't know, Holden," he said heavily, his unhappiness with his mate's reactions coloring his words. "I only know that chosen mates are supposed to be blissfully happy after mating. I know that the love and the bond that forms between mates is person-specific and has nothing to do with gender." He twisted his head so that his eyes could meet Holden's. "I know that my sex life has never been about gender. I don't have sex with people I don't and can't like no matter how attractive they might be. I've never had a painful or difficult break up with someone and I don't have exes who hate me."

Now Holden flinched and Garret wondered how many of his exes hated him. Probably all of them, he thought cynically as he reached for the door knob.

"Wait!"

At Holden's exclamation, Garret paused, about to turn the handle of the door. "What?"

"You're just gonna go down to dinner like nothing happened?"

Garret sighed again. He turned to face Holden. "Nothing did happen. And you're blowing this all out of proportion," he said quietly.

Holden's black brows rose. "Being confused and angry and upset because I've discovered I have a man for a mate when I'm not into men is blowing it out of proportion?"

The mocking incredulity on Holden's face pushed Garret over the edge. Reaching out, his hands grasped Holden by the shoulders. He yanked the heavier man close to him, his mouth finding Holden's half open one. Anger fueled the kiss. Lust was the farthest thing from his mind when he'd touched Holden. But the taste of Holden's mouth on his tongue, the rasp of the man's five o'clock shadow against his own stubbled jaw, the feel of those heavy shoulder muscles bunching beneath his fingers, served to light a fire inside Garret that he'd never felt before. He let his tongue flicker over Holden's lower lip, teasing and tasting. His hips brushed Holden's and his cock began to stir.

Holden must have felt it too because he went stiff and still. Angry with himself for his lack of control, Garret tore his mouth from Holden's and spun on the balls of his feet, reaching for the door. Without looking back, he slammed out of the suite and headed for the stairs. He pounded down the two flights and emerged in the lobby. Bypassing the restaurant, he veered into the bar and out onto the patio. He leaned against the railing, chest heaving, sucking in great gulps of cold night air.

"Sir?"

He turned his head and saw a waitress hovering. He forced a smile for her. "Scotch. Neat," he told her. "A double."

Garret looked out into the darkness as she walked away. Why the fuck he'd had to come here when he'd been perfectly happy at home in England was beyond his understanding. Alfred Stone had been persuasive, but so had every other man who'd tried to hire him in the past five years. He didn't know why he'd given in to Alfred. And once he was here and Sean had offered him the position at Antaeus International, he had no idea why he'd said yes. He didn't like to change jobs. He didn't like to move. He liked his life to be neat and safe and easy. Nothing about coming here had been easy. And now there was Holden Antaeus to make things even more difficult.

The waitress returned with his Scotch and he paid her, giving a generous tip. He leaned on the wrought iron railing and sipped his drink, unhappiness settling into the space behind his breast bone. Meeting Holden told him why he'd found himself saying yes when first Alfred and then Sean had hired him. He was meant to be here. However, he had no idea how he could fix what was wrong between them. He couldn't make Holden want him. He knew quite well that intended mates who never mated spent their lives in a hell made of unhappiness and pain.

With a sigh, he rubbed one hand over his face. For the first time in a very long time, he wasn't sure what to do. He tossed back his Scotch and set the glass on a table.

"Can I buy you another one?"

The voice belonged to a man sitting in the darkest corner of the patio. Garret took in the lean, muscular body set in a casual pose. The man's eyes gleamed in the darkness, a feral light in them. Garret knew what that light meant. He was being cruised.

"I have a business dinner to attend," he said as he shook his head.

The man stood up and Garret moved toward him. "After?" the man asked.

He had no reason to refuse, Garret thought viciously. Holden didn't want him. Didn't want to explore the possibilities raised by the fact that they were mates. Sure, it was all new and scary but the man didn't even want to accept that such a thing could happen.

It had been a long time since he'd gotten laid and the man with the blatant invitation in his eyes was hot. It wouldn't hurt to enjoy himself for once, Garret decided.

"Sure. I'll meet you back here in a couple of hours once I'm finished with business." He looked at the smile that curved the other man's lips. Damn he was hot. As he stared, the man's tongue swept out along his lower lip and Garret's groin tightened. "I'm Garret," he said, mesmerized by the movement of the pink tongue. He wondered what it would feel like on his cock.

"I'm Rob." The man reached up and brushed his fingers along the placket of Garret's khaki trousers. "I'll be waiting." He sat down at his table and saluted Garret with his drink, a sly smile playing about his lips.

Garret headed for the restaurant, his head spinning with alcohol, lust, confusion, and a good dose of pain. Holden wasn't the only one upset by circumstances, he thought angrily as he followed the hostess to a private room where the rest of the Antaeus International executives were. Luckily, they were all standing around with cocktails in hand instead of seated at the long table. He would have hated walking in late only to find them all seated and staring at him. His eyes instantly picked out Holden standing in a corner of the room, deep in conversation with his brother Declan. Briefly, he wondered if Holden had told his brother what had happened.

A hand touched his shoulder and he turned, grateful to find his boss Emily standing there in a red designer sweater and black silk slacks. "They only seem like they'll bite," she murmured in his ear.

Garret smiled. He liked Emily. There was a lot more to her than people realized. "Who exactly?" he asked in a conspiratorial whisper.

She waved her hand, the contents of the martini glass sloshing dangerously near the rim. "All of 'em. But mostly, those Antaeus brothers." Her hazel eyes narrowed then. "And Sean's brown nosed Siamese twin."

"Siamese twin?" Garret wondered if this was some colloquialism that he didn't know.

Emily nodded, her sleek blonde ponytail bobbing. "Vahid. He and Sean are like Siamese twins, attached at nose and ass. Vahid's nose to Sean's ass," she whispered.

Garret bit the inside of his mouth to stop himself from roaring with laughter. "How many of those have you had?" he asked his boss, gesturing toward her drink.

She shrugged carelessly and finished it. "Who cares? It's not my dime and I'm not the one doing all the speeches tonight. I'm entitled to get blitzed on a night like this. I lost my chance to be happy because of this job. Alcohol helps make that circumstance easier to live with."

Emily sauntered away toward the bar, balancing carefully on her spike heeled shoes. Garret's grin faded as he processed Emily's words. He would never have guessed she was so unhappy. She had a brilliant mind for finance and was a perfect corporate executive. He'd never heard anything but rave reviews for her. Getting a glimpse of her private hell made him wonder if he would end up the same. His happiness hinged on Holden's acceptance of what was meant to be. He'd never liked having things out of his control but he'd learned early on in the stock market that he had to let go and take the risks. Dealing with Holden would be a lot like playing the stocks. And at the moment, he was losing his ass...

Dinner turned out to be a boring drawn out exercise in patience and tact. Emily sat beside him getting drunker by the minute. On his other side, Vahid grew stiff with annoyance the more Emily drank. Sean's speech was like a bad spoof of motivational speakers. Far down the table from him, Holden and Declan had their heads together and were writing on napkins. Tension coiled around the back of Garret's neck and tightened his spine. He hoped like hell that Rob was gonna suck his cock because after this dinner, he needed some kind of release or he'd never get to sleep knowing that Holden was so near, yet so far from accepting him.

The moment Sean concluded the evening, Vahid grasped Emily by the elbow and hustled her limp form from the room. Holden and Declan disappeared. Sean appeared beside him, a small smile curling his firm mouth.

"The Australia takeover has issues," he said gesturing toward the seats his brothers had vacated. "Don't be surprised if Holden doesn't make it back to your suite until the wee hours." He flashed a grin then. "Are you settling in? Learning all the names?"

Garret smiled politely. "Yes. Emily's great. I'm going to enjoy working with her."

"I knew you would," Sean replied, his grin fading a little. "She'll be grooming you to take her place one day so stay sharp."

As Sean moved away toward another group of managers, Garret wondered what he meant about Emily grooming him to take her place. She was young and healthy and immortal. He couldn't see her leaving her job until she was ready to retire. Garret recalled her saying that she'd lost her chance for happiness because of her job. That didn't sound like someone who was preparing to leave. Perhaps Sean had some kind of promotion up his sleeve for her. Holden had said that Sean liked being the puppet master.

As he headed toward the bar, Garret tried to shake off his amazement that Holden had spoken those words only that morning. It seemed like a lifetime had passed in the span of a day. The discovery that Holden was his mate obviously made everything seem surreal. He paused, his footsteps slowing. A big part of him didn't want to meet Rob in the bar. Holden was his mate. That was who he wanted to fuck. The memory of that angry kiss lingered in his soul. A shiver went through him. Holden didn't want him and Garrett didn't know how to deal. Questions he had no answers for rose within him. Did he try to convince Holden? Did he leave him alone to figure it out? And meanwhile, was he supposed to be celibate? What if Holden never came around?

Garret's eyes shifted from the elevators to the bar. He barely knew Holden; although, his body recognized the man as his mate. At this point, it probably didn't matter in the least if he was faithful to Holden. The man didn't even consider them a couple, let alone mates. A flash of anger spurred him on toward the bar. On the patio, Rob's long, lean form waited.

Ignoring the waitress, Garret strode over to Rob's table. "Dinner's over."

Rob looked up and smiled, his white teeth flashing. "So I see." He reached out a hand and stroked Garret's thigh. "Do you want a drink or should we go somewhere more private?"

Arousal spiraled through Garret's body. "The coworker I'm sharing a suite with is out for a few hours on business. We can go to my suite and have a drink."

"Sounds good to me."

Rob rose to his feet, his long jean clad legs carrying him easily out of the bar and into the lobby. Garret followed and they got in an elevator. Alone in the car, Rob rubbed a hand over Garret's ass, lust filling his eyes. "You bottom?" he asked in a low tone.

Garret shrugged. "I do it all. I'm versatile," he murmured in a sardonic tone. He eyed the other man for a moment, sizing him up. Then he said in a rough voice, "but I'd like it a lot more if you were my little sub tonight. Would you like that?"

The lust on Rob's face fired brighter. His nostrils flared. The elevator door opened and Garret headed down the hotel corridor to his suite. Once inside, Rob reached for him, but Garret sidestepped out of reach. "Do you want a drink?"

Rob shook his head. "No. Are you gonna tell me what to do?"

Garret walked over to the sofa and sat down. He pointed to the space between his spread thighs. "Here," he ordered. "Naked."

Rob hurried over, pulling his t-shirt from the waistband of his jeans. The shirt landed on the coffee table. The zipper of the jeans slid down and then the denim thudded to the carpet. Garret watched with narrowed eyes as Rob removed his boots and kicked the jeans aside. By the time Rob was naked, his cock was hard. Garret noticed that it was a respectable size, curving up toward his washboard abs and belly button.

"Stroke it for me," he whispered.

With a low groan, Rob grasped his cock and began to masturbate. Pre-cum leaked from the thick head and Garret leaned forward, licking it up with a swipe of his tongue. Rob groaned and thrust his hips toward Garret. Digging his fingers into Rob's thigh muscle, Garret told him, "Kneel here between my legs."

The moment Rob was on his knees, Garret yanked the zipper down on his khakis, lifting his hips to push down his briefs and slacks. He kicked away his shoes and socks and yanked his polo shirt over his head. Spreading his thighs wider, he grabbed Rob by the back of the neck.

"Suck me."

The words were rough, growled in a belligerent tone. Frustration over his situation with Holden fueled his passion. He pushed Rob's head toward his straining cock. Mouth open, the man came at him. He licked Garret's balls and rubbed the flat of his palms over Garret's chest, tweaking his nipples. Garret's breath came harder. A low moan escaped him as Rob deep-throated his cock. The hot wet suction sent pleasure rippling through Garrett's body. He loved the feel of Rob's mouth on his cock. It had been a long time since someone had blown him, let alone so well.

His balls tightened, but he didn't want to come yet. He pushed Rob away and got to his feet, stepping away from the sofa. He stood, legs braced apart, in front of the door to the patio. Rob still knelt by the sofa, his hand rapidly stroking his thick cock. Sweat glistened on his hard body as he stared hungrily at Garret's shaft.

Garret pointed it at him. "Come and get it," he said in a low rough voice.

Rob didn't waste any time. He crawled across the carpet and engulfed Garret's cock in his mouth again. A wave of pleasure swept over Garret and he fought not to come. "Stroke your cock," he ordered.

He looked down, watching Rob's hand moving rapidly on his own turgid flesh. It was obvious to Garret that the man was going to come very soon. He buried his fingers in Rob's hair and began to fuck the man's face, at first gently, then more urgently as his orgasm neared.

Rob's tongue swirled over the underside of Garret's cock as his cheeks hollowed with each suck. Garret could feel his balls tighten, a low ache beginning in them and spreading through his groin.

"Fuck, yeah. Suck me," he growled, smoke trickling from his nostrils.

Garret closed his eyes and pretended the mouth that sucked him was Holden's. In the deepest recesses of his mind, he knew that what he was doing was wrong. For another, he knew that sex with Holden wouldn't be anything like this. This was only lust. Anything he did with Holden would feel a thousand times better by all accounts.

He pictured Holden's muscular form, imagining it naked, imagining what his cock would look like. Rob rolled his tongue over Garret's cock. Between the image of Holden's naked body and what Rob was doing to him, Garret felt his balls release as pleasure flooded his senses. He cried out as he came, his cum filling Rob's eager sucking mouth.

Then a growl of rage penetrated his orgasm-fogged brain. Garret's eyes flew open to find Holden standing in his bedroom doorway, clad only in a damp towel, his hair wet from the shower. Fury filled Holden's amber eyes making them glow eerily in the dark room. Garret jerked away from Rob, pulling his cock from the man's mouth just as Rob came, his cum spurting out onto Garret's shins.

Anger, dismay, embarrassment, and fear all vied for top honors in Garret's head. His eyes were locked on Holden who glared at Rob. Holden trembled with a fury so palpable Garret didn't know what to think. Their eyes met and Garret could see Holden's confused rage. Then Holden spun around and went back in his room, slamming the door resoundingly.

Shaking with reaction from what had just happened with Holden and from the force of his orgasm, Garret slumped onto the sofa. Rob slinked around picking up his clothes and getting dressed.

"I'll...uh...just take off now...it was...uh...nice..." His voice trailed away and a few minutes later he was gone.

Garret bolted from the couch, gathering his things and storming into his room, slamming the door behind him. Fury replaced every other emotion he'd felt. Holden was his mate, but the man didn't want to be. Yet, he'd barged in on Garret and looked at him with such rage that Garret had wanted to crawl to him on hands and knees and beg his forgiveness.

Tossing his clothes into a laundry bag, Garret got into the shower. Hot water gushed from the shower heads, steam quickly filling the bathroom. Damn him! Why did Holden have to make everything so difficult? It wasn't supposed to be like this when you found your mate. It wasn't supposed to be confusing and painful. It was supposed to be a joyous thing.

Leaning his forehead against the cool tile, Garret finally calmed and acknowledged to himself that the mating bonds were already winding their tendrils around him. He barely knew Holden and yet he felt guilty for being with Rob. He had to find a way to convince Holden that things would be great between them. Despite being straight, Holden would soon feel the same sexual pull that Garret felt and hopefully it would help ease things between them.

Turning off the shower, Garret stepped out and dried. He slipped into bed and stared at the ceiling for what seemed like hours, trying to figure out how to make Holden want him and accept a relationship. He kept seeing Emily, drinking herself into a stupor, and knew with every atom in his body that he didn't want to be that unhappy. It would be unbearable. Already his chest ached as if there was a gaping hole behind his breast bone.

He'd spent a lot of years solving problems for his employers and clients. Now he had a problem he needed to solve and he could barely think about it, let alone come up with a way to make everything right. As the moon crept higher in the night sky, he fell into a fitful sleep, resolving that he would find a way to fight for Holden Antaeus. The alternative would be to walk away and pretend the man didn't exist. Unfortunately, his heart knew differently and wasn't about to let him forget it.

Chapter Three

Holden hadn't ever felt a fury like the one lashing him now. His heart thundered louder than the slamming of his bedroom door and the reverberations rippled through his body. He yanked off the damp towel and slung it full force at a chair before tunneling beneath the covers of his bed to lay, chest heaving, in the darkness.

Confusion, fear, and anger warred inside him for top honors. He'd been off balance from the moment he'd smelled Garret's spearmint scent. Every cell in his body had told him that the man was his mate, but his head refused to wrap around the idea. It didn't seem logical to him. From the moment he'd become aware of sexual attraction, he'd always wanted women. He'd never found men sexually attractive. Yet, there had been something instantly appealing about Garret. Holden had felt a pull inside him as they'd sat in his office that morning, but he hadn't understood its meaning. Then when he'd brought things to a head with Garret before dinner, only to be told what his body seemed to already instinctively know, he'd been afraid and confused. The more Garret insisted their mating was the truth, the angrier Holden had become. He didn't want or need a complication like this in his life.

Before dinner, he'd cornered his brother Declan and drilled him about mating. Declan had told him everything he knew, which admittedly wasn't a lot because Declan wasn't mated. Holden hadn't told Declan about Garret but he knew his brother suspected something was going on. After dinner, they'd had a cigar and then Declan had left to check on the Australian takeover while Holden had returned to his suite and locked himself in his bedroom, retreating to his personal Jacuzzi tub for a long soak.

Thoughts of his conversation with Garret before dinner had come back to him as he'd let the hot water and bubbles ease his tense muscles. He'd felt the same pull inside him that Garret had said he'd felt. Holden's emotions were tumbled and confused, but they still felt connected to Garret. Fear kept him from even acknowledging that there was a sexual side to the situation. He wasn't ready to face that yet.

The rush and whoosh of the churning water in the tub had droned loudly so Holden couldn't tell if Garret had returned to the suite or not. However, when he had gotten out of the tub and had stepped into his bedroom, the sound of voices in the main room of the suite came very clearly to his ears. He'd instantly known that Garret wasn't alone and although he hadn't wanted to face the part sex played in the whole mating process, Holden had tensed with anger. A possessiveness he'd never felt before had grabbed him, fueling his march across the room. Not even thinking about the fact that he wore only a damp towel, he'd thrown open the door and been confronted with a pornographic scene. A sick feeling had taken hold of his stomach as he'd watched Garret in the throes of an orgasm. The man in front of him had his face buried in Garret's crotch, obviously sucking his cock, swallowing his cum. On top of that, the man had clearly been turned on by Garret.

Holden's gaze had taken in the man's thick erection, glistening with pre-cum. Primal emotions had flared red hot inside him and a growl escaped his control as he'd fought the urge to rip the man away from Garret. When Garret had pulled away, the man's cock was spurting onto Garret's legs. The urge to pummel the stranger into raw meat had risen inside Holden. For an instant, he'd locked gazes with Garret. In his new mate's eyes, he'd seen regret and pain before Holden realized he literally shook with fury. Spinning around, intent on escaping the sight, sound, and scent of the men's sex, he'd slammed his bedroom door shut.

Holden lay between the soft sheets, his body wreathed in heat, his mind in turmoil, and he had no idea what to do. His life had suddenly become a mess. A huge flaming mess, he thought angrily. And apparently, he was the flamer.

Holden had known gay men in his ninety years of existence, but he'd never seen men have sex. Although, he sorta knew what they did together. Well, he did know what they did together, but he'd never given it much thought since it wasn't his thing. Now, as much as he didn't want to think about it, images of a naked Garret with his cock in that man's mouth refused to leave Holden's brain. Layered with the rush of emotion and sensation he'd felt when Garret had kissed him earlier, it was all more than Holden could take.

This morning he'd been a normal heterosexual man with a demanding girlfriend whose mouth drove him insane with pleasure. Now, at midnight, he tossed and turned in his bed, thinking about the rasp of a man's stubbled jaw against his own, the taste of his firm lips and agile tongue, and how a wave of pure lust had swept over him when he'd seen the man naked. Already the emotional bonds of mating pulled at him. If they hadn't been, he wouldn't have wanted to kill the man who was naked with Garret.

With a heavy sigh, Holden rolled onto his stomach, half surprised to find that his cock was semi-erect. He flexed his hips, rubbing his erection against the sheets as he hugged the pillow, burying his face in its softness. What was happening to him wasn't even something he could talk to Declan about, and usually he talked to his older brother about everything. For a moment, he contemplated calling Eden because she always had an open, non-judgmental ear. However, the dilemma he found himself in this time would not go away even if he spilled his guts to his sister. Nothing any of his siblings could say to him would fix what had happened. He would be forced to accept Garret as his mate whether he was comfortable with it or not. And according to his cock, which now throbbed with lust, he was becoming more used to the idea by the moment.

Closing his eyes, he rubbed his cock against the sheets, the rhythmic sensation making him groggy. As he drifted to sleep, he decided that confusion notwithstanding, he didn't want to be unhappy. He'd heard horrible things about dragons not completing the mating process with their chosen mate. Somehow, he had to find a way to accept what had happened. The first step had to be getting to know Garret. Everything seemed so surreal. If he spent some time with Garret and got to know the man, maybe his emotions and his head would sync up, making the whole mating process a lot easier to swallow. So, tomorrow, he would work on getting to know Garret.

~* * *~

The sun barely peeped over the horizon when Holden woke with a jerk. He lay on his back, spread eagle, the covers kicked off and his skin drenched in sweat. Pools of semen decorated his taut abdomen and chest.

"Holy fuck," he muttered in disgust. He hadn't had a wet dream in more than seventy years. In his youth, sex had dominated his thoughts and dreams. As he'd grown and matured, gaining more control over his thoughts and emotions, his sexual dreams had become fewer and fewer until they'd disappeared altogether.

Holden got up and headed for the shower. As he washed, he tried to recall the dream, but all he got were visions of Garret's naked body as his cock slid from the mouth of the man who'd been sucking it so avidly. Hot water sluiced over him and Holden closed his eyes wondering what it would feel like to touch the long lean slabs of muscle that covered Garret's frame. He wondered what it would feel like to have Garret touch him. He'd never thought men attractive before, but he realized that Garret was exceptionally handsome. With his open minded sexuality, he had to have been with quite a few men and women.

Pushing aside his sexual thoughts, Holden stepped out of the shower and dressed quickly in shorts and a t-shirt. He opened his bedroom door and the stale scent of sex assaulted him. With a growl, he let a burst of dragonfire escape him, a small fireball not big enough to set the room on fire, but enough to burn off the smell of that other man's cum. The acrid scent of smoke permeated the room now, and Holden strode over to the wet bar, yanking open the small refrigerator. He grabbed a bottle of water and drank half of it in a couple of gulps. Calm settled along his nerve endings and he set the water on the counter, crossing the room to Garret's bedroom.

Knocking softly, he opened the door. Sprawled on his side, one foot sticking out from beneath the sheet, the sleeping Garret's wide shoulders seemed pale against the navy colored cotton sheets. As Holden watched, he rolled onto his back, his eyes slitting open. The navy sheet rode low against his hips and Holden's eyes were drawn to the finely sculpted muscles of Garret's body. Although taller than Holden, Garret had long smooth muscles and a leaner body mass. A fine dusting of pale brown hair decorated his pecs and arrowed down his abdomen to disappear beneath the blue sheet.

"Get up," Holden said softly. "The tennis courts are empty at dawn."

Garret's eyes widened in surprise and Holden could see the suppressed emotion in them. "Is that an order or are you asking me?" Garret croaked in a sleep roughed voice.

His caution didn't surprise Holden. With a wry smile, he turned toward the door. "It's not an order, but I'm not asking either. If we're going to figure this out, we need to get to know each other. That means you get your stiff British rump out of bed and join me on the tennis court. After we play, we'll have breakfast and talk. We should have time to shower before Sean's first workshop of the day."

Holden wanted to look over his shoulder to see Garret's reaction. He didn't. He returned to the main room of the suite and picked up his water, wandering out to the balcony to watch the sun rise. It couldn't have been more than ten minutes later that he heard a soft sound that told him Garret had joined him.

"Holden, I'm sorry."

The softly spoken words caused Holden to release his breath on a sigh. "I am too, Garret." He turned, his gaze caught and held by Garret's. A wave of emotion, mostly indefinable, rose within him, causing an ache in his chest.

Garret swallowed, his Adam's apple bobbing slightly. "I shouldn't have done that."

Holden sensed Garret's discomfort, but stayed silent, waiting for him to finish. He gave the man points for holding his gaze when by rights he probably wanted to look anywhere else.

"I was angry and disappointed and confused. When Rob came on to me in the bar..." Garret broke off and swallowed again. "I didn't think you would care what I did, but that is no excuse. It's just an explanation of my motivation. I know it was wrong of me to bring him back here on the day I found you. I'm so sorry."

It had been a long time since Holden had met someone with the level of integrity that Garret had just shown. "I'm sorry too, Garret," he replied in a low voice. "This whole thing was such a shock. And I know that's not an excuse for my behavior. It's just an explanation."

He smiled as he repeated Garret's words. The British man's eyes lightened as a smile curved his lips. Holden caught a glimpse of brilliant white teeth as Garret's smile flashed out and he suddenly felt sucker punched, his gut twisting with emotion. The urge to reach out and touch Garret overwhelmed him, just like the man's scent filled his senses, until all he could think about was asking him to repeat yesterday's kiss.

Garret's eyes flickered. "You realize that a lot of what you think and feel bleeds out to me now," he murmured. "Despite your natural shielding."

Holden sucked in a breath. "If you know what I'm thinking then just do it, Garret, 'cause the gods know I can't yet," he said in a shaky voice, feeling his heart begin to race.

Garret took the three steps needed to bring their bodies within inches of each other. Holden began to shake a little with fear and anticipation. The first kiss had been a surprise and filled with anger on both sides. This would be their first real kiss. They both acknowledged that they were mates, and that they felt some emotion pulling at them along with a steadily growing attraction. Regardless of the previous kiss, Holden didn't know what to expect and when Garret's hand came up to wrap around the back of his neck, he stiffened a little at first. Then fire licked through his veins at the feel of Garret's warm palm on his bare skin. He shook harder.

"Don't be afraid, Holden. It's just a kiss."

Garret's soft whisper accompanied the press of his thumb against the underside of Holden's jaw. Reflexively, he tilted his chin up and Garret's mouth came down on his. Lust swept through his body as Garret expertly parted his lips. Holden gasped a little opening his mouth wider as Garret's tongue glided easily against his own, the wet heat sending lightning bolts of desire shooting through him. This time when Garret's hips brushed his, he didn't move, letting the man press his growing erection against him. His own cock started to respond, twitching inside his shorts.

Just as Holden was about to let go and kiss Garret back, the British man broke off the kiss on a long shuddering sigh. "I think we need to go downstairs before I forget that you've never been with a man before, Holden," he said in a shaken voice.

Garret took a step back and Holden took in the stormy green eyes, the wetness of his full bottom lip, and the erection that strained the front of his navy cotton shorts. The broad shoulders covered in a pale blue polo shirt shook a little with his efforts to control his rapid breathing. Holden felt as shaken as Garret appeared. He knew his black t-shirt did nothing to hide his rapid breathing nor did his grey sweat shorts hide the fact that his cock had hardened.

"I don't know how we're going to work this out, Garret, but I don't want to be unhappy either. I don't know why you're my mate, but maybe as we get to know each other that will become clear." Holden's confession spilled from his lips, causing Garret's eyes to widen in surprise. "I know nothing about being with a man and what I'm beginning to feel for you scares me. I've been with a lot of women, but that doesn't tell me how to do... *this*."

Garret's mouth curved in a reassuring smile that made Holden feel better the instant he saw it. "Holden, I've been with a lot of women *and* men, but I don't know how to do mates either. Sure, I know how to kiss a man, how to suck his cock, how to fuck him, and how to let him fuck me, but that doesn't mean I know how do those things with someone who is the most important person in the world to me. Because, Holden..."

He broke off and reached out to take Holden's hand in his for a moment. "You are now the most important person in my life and we both need to learn how to deal with that."

Holden nodded and Garret dropped his hand. "Did you bring a racket?" Holden asked gruffly.

"Yeah. I'll get it." Garret flashed another of those brilliant smiles that Holden felt in every nerve ending.

As Garret stepped back into the suite, Holden reached for his water bottle with a shaky hand. Dear gods. He was actually going to go through with this whole thing. He actually had accepted the fact that he had a male mate. Well, as much as he could accept it at the moment. If Garret had touched his cock, Holden probably would have freaked out. He accepted that desire for Garret had begun to wrap it's tendrils around him, but he wasn't ready to get naked with the man. The thought still sort of squicked him out. He couldn't imagine himself touching another man's cock, let alone sucking it. Although, fucking might not be too hard to do. After all, Holden had always loved anal sex.

For the first time, he thought about what would be required of him having a male mate. He'd always loved having his cock sucked but now, it would be Garret sucking it, not a woman. He'd always loved having anal sex, but now he would fuck Garret's ass, not a woman's. When he slid his cock deep inside the tight ring of anal muscles, it would be Garret's cock his fingers would seek, not the wet swollen nub of a woman's clit. A frisson of fear went down his spine and he finished the bottle of water in one long swallow. This might not be easy at all, he thought as he headed to his room to get his racket.

When he returned, he found Garret near the door, waiting patiently with a hooded expression. He figured his thoughts were bleeding out again.

"I'm not ready to talk sex yet," he said stiffly as he opened the door. "Maybe tonight. Today, let's just get to know each other. A game of tennis, some breakfast, and then Sean's group activity for the day. After that, we can grab some lunch and get into the strategy session Sean wants."

"Then maybe a swim before dinner?" Garret suggested.

Holden nodded. "Sounds good to me."

The tennis courts were indeed empty at that hour. Garret turned out to be a good player, although not in Holden's league, but he held his own pretty well which pleased Holden. At breakfast, they discovered they both liked their bagels with butter, not cream cheese, and preferred bacon over sausage. They both had a love of good strong coffee, but where Garret doused his with cream and sugar, Holden liked his black. When Holden asked Garret about drinking tea, the Englishman made a face, saying that not all Brits liked tea.

They both disliked politics, but the state of the economy interested both of them albeit for different reasons. Garret kept his fingers on the pulse of the stock market, which meant that he was intensely interested in the economy and current trends. Holden stayed abreast of economic trends because he and Declan were always on the lookout for businesses they could buy to increase Antaeus Internationals profits and net worth.

After breakfast, they returned to their suite to shower and dress for the seminar Sean had planned. As he stood in the shower, Holden got an image of Garret in his shower, stroking his cock. He shivered, knowing that if Garret was masturbating, the man had to be fantasizing about him. The thought aroused him, but he still wasn't at the point where he could fantasize about being with Garret sexually. Sex with a man, even when the man was Garret, still seemed completely alien to him.

They met in the main room of the suite before heading down to the seminar. Garret was dressed in dark slacks and a pale yellow polo shirt. Holden wore dark jeans and a plain white button down shirt. He eyed Garret's shiny loafers then flicked a glance at his own beat up runners. Of course, Garret was new to the company and still dressing to impress. As one of the owners of the company, Holden could dress as he pleased.

Still, it amused him a little that the bean counter looked all shiny and spiffy.

"I'm not a bean counter," Garret protested in a low growl as they headed down to the lodge's conference room in the elevator.

Holden made a rude sound. "You're a finance whiz kid. That means you're a bean counter," he teased.

Garret's emerald eyes flashed. "You'll pay for that later, Holden."

"Really?" Holden held open the door to the conference room. "I'm all agog to know how."

A sly smile curved Garret's mobile mouth. "No, you aren't. You're not ready to go there yet. But I'm hopeful that you will be soon."

Heat flashed through Holden's body as he had a sudden vision of Garret kneeling between his thighs reaching for his cock. His eyes met Garret's and he realized the other man had sent him the thought. Before he could reply, Emily appeared and took Garret by the arm dragging him across the room.

Biting back a sigh, Holden looked for his brothers and found Declan with Vahid in a corner of the room. Sean was nowhere in sight. As he walked up to Declan, he heard Vahid hiss, "I'm not Emily's keeper. I can't stop her from drinking!"

Holden's brows rose a little and his eyes met his older brother's. Vahid never got angry. Even when their sister Eden had dumped him, Vahid hadn't shown anger. His palpable annoyance made Holden wonder what the hell Emily had done to him. He decided to help Vahid out a little.

"He's right, Declan. Let him be. Emily's responsible for her own behavior. Just because Vahid always makes everything perfect for Sean doesn't mean he can control all of us," Holden teased with a wink.

Vahid's smile was patently false but he nodded at Holden's words and used the distraction to slip away. Holden snagged his older brother's gaze. "Picking on Vahid? Are you pissed at Sean?" he said with a wry smile.

Declan let out a weary sigh. "No. But usually Vahid makes sure everything runs smoothly. Last night, he sat back and let Emily make a fool of herself. He would not have done that with any other executive in the company," he explained. "He would have told the bartender to water their drinks or not serve them anymore. I don't know why he picked on her last night. I asked him if they'd had a fight over the budget or something and he wouldn't answer."

Holden shook his head in surprise. "That is unusual for Vahid. She must have done something to put his panties in a twist."

Declan nodded his agreement. "And how about you? Yesterday you were all bent out of shape about being paired with Wonderboy and today you show up almost arm in arm. What gives?"

Holden shrugged as they moved toward their seats at the conference table. "We played tennis this morning. He's good."

A laugh escaped Declan. "I get it. You're just happy to have someone to play with again. The noob doesn't realize he has no chance of ever winning against you."

The vision of Garret sucking his cock flashed through Holden's mind again and his lips twitched into a smile. "Oh, I wouldn't say that. He's got some moves neither of us ever anticipated."

Declan looked at him with a puzzled frown, but Holden just smiled and opened his portfolio as Sean came into the room with the day's speaker.

Chapter Four

Garret's hopes for a private lunch with Holden were dashed when Vahid and Sean decided to join them. Similarly, their strategy session ended up including Emily and Declan. Garret tried not to be disappointed because business was business after all, yet he couldn't help but feel a little impatient that his time alone with Holden had been invaded.

He'd been hugely relieved that his actions the night before hadn't spoiled the promise of a relationship with Holden. In fact, they seemed to have spurred his new mate into some hard thoughts about mating and the future. Anything that served to open Holden's mind to the truth and the possibilities was fine by Garret.

The kiss they'd shared on the balcony had been the hottest kiss of Garret's life. His senses were becoming tuned to Holden's and he'd known right when things had started to shift toward out of control. He'd already decided that he needed to take things slowly with Holden. His new mate was freaked by the thought of sex with a man. Garret knew he had to back off in spite of the fact Holden had been on the verge of kissing him back. At least Holden hadn't been afraid of Garret's erection this time. Pressing his cock against Holden's crotch and feeling the man's own cock respond had sent shivers of delight and lust through Garret. He couldn't wait to touch Holden's naked body. Touch and taste it.

The strategy session didn't drag as Garret had thought it would. He discovered that Holden and Declan Antaeus worked together like a well-oiled machine. Declan excelled at choosing a target company to take over. Holden excelled at knowing the legal issues they faced. Coupled with Emily's brilliance when it came to knowing the value and worth of a company, the three of them managed a takeover or buyout with a smooth professionalism that awed Garret.

It dawned on him that he'd joined a company run by a group of supremely intelligent and professional executives. None of these people rested on their laurels or let their underlings do all the work. They were dedicated and brilliant at what they did. It made him glad he'd decided to take Sean's offer. A company like this gave him something he could sink his teeth into.

When the strategy session finished, Declan and Holden headed for the business center of the lodge intent on faxing yet another sheaf of documents to Australia. Garret stood watching them walk away, both tall, dark-haired, and athletic, although Declan stood a good three inches taller than Holden. Still, they were attractive men and obviously related. As they disappeared from view, Garret wondered what it would be like to be part of the Antaeus family.

"Don't let them eat you alive," Emily advised with a lift of her perfectly plucked eyebrows. "I can see how much their business acumen turns you on. Just don't let them use you, Garret."

"I won't," he responded easily, giving her a reassuring smile.

She patted his arm. "Good. I'll see you tomorrow."

Garret looked at her in surprise. "You're not coming down to dinner?"

"It's not a group dinner night. I'm going to visit the spa and call room service. If I don't spoil me, no one will," she told him, her voice tinged with bitterness again. "You have a good night."

Garret stared after Emily's elegant form. Her bitterness was obviously not new. The cool control he'd observed in her up until now must have undergone some massive meltdown. He couldn't imagine what would make an accomplished executive like Emily Carrington crack.

He headed up to his suite and changed for the swim that he and Holden had planned. Standing in front of the full length closet mirror, he eyed himself critically. For a hundred and twenty-year-old dragon, he looked pretty good. No gray in his dark hair yet, nor wrinkles, although he did have a crinkle between his brows from frowning. He looked like a human male in his early thirties until one noticed the dragon clan mark that twisted across his lower back.

The black swirling lines were often mistaken for a tattoo and he'd been teased about having a "tramp stamp." The single black dragon with an emerald in its mouth had etched itself on his skin when he'd come of age sexually. The emerald was the only part of the mark that wasn't black. As he stared in the mirror at his clan mark, he remembered seeing Holden's clan mark the night before. When he'd turned and slammed his door, Garret had gotten a glimpse of lines running down his spine between his shoulder blades.

Garret knew his looks didn't even compare to Holden's. His chestnut brown hair and green eyes were not as dramatic as Holden's ink black hair and bright amber eyes. Even their physiques weren't comparable. Holden had a sleek hairless chest while Garret had his little fur patch and a trail of hair down his abdomen. Regardless of the fact that he had a lean, taut swimmer's body with defined muscles, Garret knew he looked nothing like the beautiful golden skinned Holden with his perfect athlete's body, bulging with sleek muscle in his biceps, shoulders, pecs, and thighs. He wasn't overly muscular like a body builder, but he wasn't as lean as Garret either.

The clan mark on Garret's lower back prickled. He turned away from the mirror, closing the closet as the sound of the suite's outer door reached his ears. He'd only taken a couple of steps toward his door when Holden appeared. Their gazes met.

"I was afraid you'd forgotten our swim," Holden said in a low voice as his attention flickered over Garret's nearly naked body in a pair of green swim shorts.

Garret's heart thundered in his chest, hoping that Holden didn't think he looked like a pasty faced Englishman, even though that description did fit him.

A grin turned up the corners of Holden's mouth as he stepped into the bedroom. "No, it doesn't. You're a little pale, but certainly not pasty faced," he said on a chuckle.

Garret's eyes opened wide with shock. Holden had heard his thoughts.

With a snort, Holden came to a stop in front of him. "You're not the only one fine tuning this mating stuff," he explained. "I've been working on it all afternoon, trying to hear you. It gets stronger the more I try."

"It gets much easier after sex," Garret said, then could have bitten his tongue out. "Or so I hear."

Holden laughed, his eyes glittering with amusement. "I've heard that too. I remember Sean saying it after he met Careen." He sobered then, his face falling into more serious lines. "This isn't easy for me, Garret, but I'm willing to work on it. I still don't understand why things shook out this way for me, for us. There must be a reason, but I guess we just don't know what it is yet. For now, let's go have that swim and then dinner here in the suite, okay?"

A surge of joy rushed through Garret at the thought of an evening alone with Holden. Already, the man commanded his emotions with as little as a flick of his eyebrow. He would do anything to have Holden touch him.

Amber eyes lit with an indefinable emotion. "We need to talk about the obvious, Garret. I don't have any practical experience when it comes to sex with a man and I'm not sure yet that I can even do it. But I'm willing to discuss it and this whole mating thing after dinner."

Garret nodded. He would have to be content with that. The gods knew he couldn't afford to push this man and lose him. "Thank you," he said quietly, grateful that Holden wasn't still freaking out.

"Oh, I'm past the freak out part and on to the 'Oh my gods. Can I do this and do I even want to?' part," Holden replied with a tense little chuckle. Then he did something that completely shocked Garret.

Holden reached out and traced his fingers over Garret's collarbone. Sucking in a breath, Garret looked into his mate's amber eyes. Little flames flickered in their depths. Holden took another step closer and his mouth sought Garret's. With a growl, Garret surrendered to Holden's kiss.

Tentative at first, as if Holden had never kissed anyone before, the softness of his lips surprised Garret. Then his natural arrogance must have come to his aid because his hands reached up to capture Garret's head between them as he deepened the kiss. Holden's tongue swept possessively into Garret's mouth, stroking boldly against his tongue and teeth. Garret's knees went weak as the passion in Holden's kiss sent pleasure crashing through him.

This time Holden's hips boldly rubbed his and Garret could feel the hard ridge of his mate's cock pressing urgently against him. His own cock responded fiercely, arcing toward his belly button and bumping against Holden's. A shiver went through them both at the contact and Garret's head filled with visions of letting Holden push him down on the bed and strip the shorts from his body.

As Garret reached for the waistband of his shorts, ready to shed them so that he could be fucked, Holden's hands gripped his wrists, stopping him. His eyes popped open as Holden broke the kiss, his chest heaving.

"No, Garret." Holden shook his head. "I'm not going to fuck you. It doesn't feel right yet."

Disappointed, Garret nodded, his hands falling away from Holden's. "You're right."

A wry smile tilted the corner of Holden's mouth. "It's not that I don't want to. I had the vision straight from your head of what it would be like to take you, and it didn't turn me off surprisingly. I just don't think I'm there yet. We're not there yet. We're still getting used to the idea of being mates. This is a big adjustment for me, to have my body want a man's—"

He broke off, confusion and embarrassment tingeing his cheekbones a slight pink. Instantly, Garret wanted to comfort him. He hadn't thought about how embarrassing it might be for a straight man to have to admit to wanting sex with another man.

Holden turned away. "Let me change and get a towel. Then we'll head down to the pool."

When Holden went into his room and shut the door, Garret sat shakily on the edge of his bed. His cock throbbed with need just as it had in the shower that morning. He didn't want to jack off yet again but his reaction to Holden's touch and kiss wasn't something he could control.

Garret wondered how the hell he would make it through an hour of swimming in a public place while both of them were dressed in skimpy shorts followed by dinner alone in the suite talking about having sex, when Holden didn't know how and didn't exactly think he could face it yet.

That thought sobered Garret and his cock responded accordingly, his erection flagging. Mating with a man who'd only been with women was equal parts joy and nightmare. Garret was already falling in love with Holden. He couldn't imagine a more attractive man if he tried. The wall in his office proved his intelligence and athletic ability. The photos on his desk showed him to be a family man who cared about his siblings and their children. In spite of their rocky start and his fear and confusion, Holden had shifted gears fairly quickly and seemed willing to give their mating a chance. Now, Garret had to do everything in his power to put his mate at ease and show him that things could be good between them.

With his cock and his thoughts firmly in control, Garret grabbed a towel from the bathroom and walked into the main room of the suite just as Holden emerged from his bedroom. Garret's breath caught in his throat. Holden Antaeus in a pair of black swim shorts had to be the most beautiful thing he'd ever seen. The man's golden skin covered muscles that rippled when he moved, testing Garret's control once more. He noticed that the body he already worshipped was practically hairless, with inky tufts at Holden's arm pits and swirls on his lower legs.

One black brow arched up in a sardonic expression. "Control, Garret..."

Blinking rapidly to free himself from the sexual haze that had come over him at the sight of Holden's nearly naked body, Garret swallowed hard and drew a deep breath. "This is tough, Holden," he admitted. "I want you. The tugging inside me is incessant and undeniable."

Holden came toward him, his towel slung over one broad, muscular shoulder. "I feel it too, Garret. And frankly, it's pretty scary," he said on a sigh. "We'll talk about it after dinner though. Right now, we both need to relax and not think about it."

Garret nodded his agreement and followed Holden from the suite. As they walked down to the pool, Garret studied the lines of Holden's clan mark. The black dragon swirled down Holden's spine from between his shoulder blades to the small of his back. Garret wondered what that mark would look like after they mated. In fact, he wondered what his own mark would look like after they did the deed.

"You're leaking out to me, Garret." Holden's voice seemed stern, but when he glanced back over his shoulder, Garret saw the wry smile on his face.

"I'm sorry. I keep trying to think of something else, but it's difficult."

Holden tossed his towel down on a lounger and kicked off his flip flops. Garret did the same, walking over to test the water temperature with his foot. The next thing he knew, he was flying through the air, tumbling into the deep end of the pool. He kicked himself back up to the surface, shaking his wet head and coughing a little. Treading water, he looked around for Holden but didn't see him. Wiping water from his eyes, he stared toward the spot he'd been standing only moments before.

Something brushed his thigh and he looked down, but then warm hands stroked over his shoulders and he felt the brush of what could only be lips on the back of his neck. Shivering, he felt Holden's body pressing against his back under the water. The sensuous feel of wet skin on skin did nothing to take his mind off mating Holden. He could swear he felt the hard ridge of the black dragon's erection rubbing against the crease of his ass.

"Later."

That one word whispered in his ear in a low, deep tone had Garret shaking with reaction. He knew Holden must have known it too. But then the hands on his shoulders stopped caressing and turned hard, pressing him down beneath the water again. This time when he came up, Holden was five feet away and laughing.

Determined that he wouldn't be caught off guard again, he began to swim laps, his arms and legs carrying him powerfully across the pool. He hit the end, tucked and spun, pushing off the side with his feet heading toward the opposite side of the pool. When he'd done fifty laps he stopped, looking around for Holden.

The black dragon sat on the edge of the pool, long legs dangling in the water, watching Garret with enigmatic golden eyes. "You do that rather effortlessly, you know. You make it look easy and I know it's not," he said.

Garret felt the corner of his mouth turn up in a wry smile. "You have your tennis trophies. Mine are for swimming."

Holden's golden eyes gleamed. "With those long lean muscles, I would have taken you for a track star."

"I tried, but let's just say that I'm a lot more graceful in the water than I am on land," he joked.

When they got back to the suite, they ordered room service and went to their respective rooms for showers. Garret tried not to think about the fact that Holden's remark about his muscles meant that the man had been looking at him. He also tried not to think about the feel of

Holden's body pressed against his back, Holden's cock rubbing his ass. Their discussion about sex and mating would happen soon enough and Garret was hopeful that it would lead to something more.

By the time he padded barefoot into the sitting room dressed in jeans and a t-shirt, Holden had already poured them each a glass of wine. It amused him that they were dressed similarly, although Holden wore jeans so well worn that they had a couple of quarter sized threadbare patches at the knees and were nearly white in color. Still, the soft denim hugged the curves of his tight ass and long legs in a way that made Garret drool.

They didn't have a chance to do more than take a sip of wine before room service arrived. The waiters set the table and laid out the food, leaving the cart beside the door. Holden handed them a tip and told them he'd put the dirty dish laden cart in the corridor when they were done.

As Garret sat down and shook out a linen napkin, he shot Holden a laughing glance. "At least with a man for a mate you don't have to worry about pulling out chairs or holding doors," he teased.

Holden sat down abruptly and just stared at Garret for a long moment. Then he picked up his napkin and placed it carefully on his lap. "So one of us isn't the female in this relationship?" he asked in a carefully neutral tone that Garret knew hid his feelings.

"You mean the fuck*ee* as opposed to the fuck*er*?" Garret kept his voice as neutral as Holden's, reaching for his knife and fork and cutting into his prime rib with studied care. When Holden didn't reply, he looked up to find the man staring at him with stormy, almost angry eyes.

With a sigh, Garret set his utensils down. "Holden, relationships between men are not like relationships between men and women," he said hoping like hell he didn't sound all preachy. "Some gay relationships are like male-female relationships because some men like being feminine. In my experiences with other bisexual men, those lines were never drawn. Most of the men I've been with have just had very open sexual attitudes. They just did what felt good without assigning a gender or stereotype to it."

Holden reached for his wine, downing half the glass, a sure giveaway to Garret that he was nervous. "You've been fucked by men before." The words were a statement. Garret had already let Holden know that he wanted to be fucked.

"Yes, I have had anal sex with men, both giving and receiving. It's a very intense experience on either end," he replied calmly, his eyes never leaving Holden's. "I have also had oral sex with men, both giving and receiving. I've fucked a lot of women too, in their pussies, in their asses and in their mouths. I'm a hundred and twenty years old, Holden. I've had a lot of sex in my life."

"I hear a *but* in there," Holden said, finishing his glass of wine.

Garret nodded. "Because there is one. I may have had a lot of sex in my life with both genders, and a number of species, but that doesn't mean I know what it's going to be like with you. Every person is unique, which makes every sexual experience unique. And this isn't exactly about sex. This is mating, Holden."

He leaned forward, his dinner forgotten, everything falling by the wayside in his need to explain how he felt to his mate. "I want to mate you, Holden. I want to touch you and be touched by you. I want to suck you and have you suck me. I want you to fuck me and, some day, I hope to be able to fuck you too. I know this is a lot to take in, but it's the truth. Already, I feel the mating bonds pulling at me, but more than that, when I see you working with your brother, when I smell your crisp lime scent, when I hear your laugh, I can tell that I am falling in love with you."

Holden blinked and sat back in his chair, his expression stunned. Irritated, Garret took a swallow of wine and tried to get a grip on his raging emotions. "I know it's quick, but I suppose that's because of the mating bonds. Still, I cannot deny what I feel. I'm beginning to love you and if this somehow doesn't work out and you walk away, it won't stop me from continuing to love you because Holden, I've never felt like this before and I don't think I ever will again."

Garret knew his voice shook with emotion. Hell, his whole body shook with the force of his confession. The feelings inside him were new and growing, but he was positive he'd fallen in love with Holden. The man was so beautiful, inside and out, that Garret couldn't help but love him. Even if Holden hadn't been his mate, Garret had the sense that he would have fallen for him.

His eyes widened then as Holden pushed away from the table and stood up. Heart pounding with fear, he looked up into those golden eyes and let Holden see everything he felt in his heart. He was Holden's. What the man chose to do with him now was anyone's guess.

Chapter Five

Holden's emotions were in turmoil. He and Garret had been at the resort for more than twenty four hours now, but at Garret's words, Holden's emotions became even more tumultuous. The word *love* falling from Garret's lips had made Holden's heart contract in his chest. Holden realized the man spoke the truth. The mating bonds had been pulling at him too. If it weren't for those feelings, he didn't know if he could have come as far as he had in accepting Garret as his mate. Listening to Garret's words, that he'd fucked and been fucked, sucked and been sucked, and that he'd had sex with women too, conjured images that set Holden on fire.

The moment Garret had said *love*, Holden knew that what he had begun to feel for Garret might be the same thing. The man's aesthetic beauty, his sexy accent, the brilliant flashing smile that seared it's way right down to Holden's toes...when combined with a rapier wit and sharply intelligent mind it was no wonder looking at him and smelling him turned Holden's insides to mush. And even worse than that, Holden had gotten an instant hard on when he'd seen Garret's clan mark, the dragon with the emerald in its mouth. To cover his reaction, he'd pushed Garret into the pool. Then, unable to stop himself, he'd dived in after him and come up from behind, stroking Garret's shoulder and instinctively pressing his hard cock into the crease of Garret's ass.

Now, looking down into Garret's worried eyes, he knew what was going to happen next even if Garret didn't. He wasn't sure yet how far he could go, or how much he could handle, but he knew he couldn't let Garret continue to think that he would turn away from him.

"Come here," he said softly, his eyes locked with Garret's.

When Garret cautiously got to his feet, Holden turned and walked into his bedroom. Behind him, he heard Garret's strangled gasp. He sat on the side of his bed and looked up as Garret hovered in the doorway, his luminous eyes dark with emotion.

"I said come here," he repeated, but this time he gestured to the space in front of him. As Garret moved slowly toward him, Holden reached down and grabbed the hem of his t-shirt, pulling the shirt over his head.

Garret's eyes flickered, but he didn't say a word as he came to a stop, his knees brushing Holden's. The touch, even between layers of denim, seared Holden. "On your knees," he murmured. "So I can kiss you."

The instant Garret knelt, Holden grabbed him by the back of the head, dragging him closer. Garret's mouth opened beneath the onslaught of Holden's rough kiss. Never would he have kissed a woman like this, his tongue twisting insistently around the other man's, his lips hard and demanding. Garret's hands slid up the planes of Holden's chest, stopping to tease his nipples. Holden knew his nipples were sensitive but Garret touching them was as if he'd been zapped by a cattle prod. Bolts of electricity crackled through his body and his dragon came to glorious life inside him, roaring with approval.

Holden pulled at Garret's t-shirt, sliding his hands beneath the material to touch the hot flesh beneath. He'd never touched a man sexually before, didn't know what it felt like to stroke muscle and bone instead of soft curved flesh. Touching Garret set fire to his senses. His fingertips tested the texture of Garret's skin as he stroked his hands over rock hard abs and firm pecs. The hair roughened patches felt alien, though not in a bad way.

Breaking the kiss, Holden stared at his mate for a moment. Garret's pale face had a slight sexual flush and the pupils of his eyes had elongated. Holden figured his own irises were slits now too. Smoke curled around them, coming from both their nostrils. Reaching down Holden tugged Garret's shirt over his head.

"Fuck. You're the most beautiful man I've ever seen," he muttered. "Your skin is like vellum." He ran his fingertips over Garret's biceps. "So pale and the texture so smooth and fine, I just want to lick you."

"Then do it," Garret rasped. "Do whatever you want to me, Holden. I belong to you."

Holden shook his head. "No. This is a two way street, Garret. We're mates. We belong to each other." He drew a shaky breath. "I don't know how far I can go right now. Already everything feels so strange that I'm fighting the urge to run. But I want to be with you. I want to try."

Garret smiled then and Holden felt the odd sensation in his gut again. The man's smile did funny things to him that he couldn't put a name to. Garret stroked his hands over Holden's chest and shoulders, his fingers raising goose bumps and setting Holden's senses on fire.

"Let's start easy then, why don't we?" Garret said quietly.

His hands stroked down Holden's ridged abdomen. Cock stiffening, Holden leaned back on his elbows, giving Garret a perfect view of the bulge behind his button fly. Without looking away from Holden's gaze, Garret rubbed the flat of his palm over the ridge in Holden's jeans.

A low moan escaped Holden and Garret popped the buttons of the jeans. He grasped the waistband of the jeans and Holden's briefs with his agile fingers and started to pull them down. Holden hissed in a breath and Garret stopped, their eyes meeting.

"What do you want, Holden?"

Lust and fear warred inside Holden. There were other emotions too, but he didn't think he could go there at the moment. Not when his cock was throbbing with need. He swallowed hard and gave voice to the visions inside his head.

"I want you to suck my cock."

Garret's smile flashed out again, this time with a gleam of triumph in it. "Then relax. You've had blow jobs before. This isn't much different."

"A blow job's a blow job, isn't it?" Holden growled, just wanting the ache in his balls to ease.

Garret winked at him. "Almost. There's something about the way a man sucks cock that tells you he knows what you're feeling."

As Garret spoke, he eased Holden's jeans and briefs from his body, prodding him with a finger to the thigh to make him lift his hips. Naked now, his thick cock curving toward his belly, pre-cum already leaking in a steady stream from the wide head, Holden's breath came in rough pants. His dragon wanted him to shove his cock at Garret, demanding he suck it, but Holden was cautious. Never having been with a man, he wasn't exactly sure what to expect. What he didn't expect was Garret to ignore his cock and get to his feet.

He watched with wide eyes as Garret unzipped his jeans and slid them down his thighs. Then he hooked his thumbs in the waistband of his briefs and pushed them down. Naked, his long, thick cock bobbing as he shifted foot-to-foot, Garret's eyes were hooded, his expression guarded. Holden gazed at the blue veined cock and heavy balls that made up Garret's genitalia. The urge to touch them grew inside him until smoke poured from his nostrils. Fear kept his hands on the bed though.

Holden spread his thighs, silently inviting Garret to touch him. With a little growl, Garret knelt on the floor at the edge of the bed, his shoulders pressing Holden's thighs wider. He blew a stream of warm air on Holden's balls and they tightened.

"You manscape," Garret said in a low voice.

"Wax. Not all of it, just some. You do too," Holden grunted, lust holding him in such an unrelenting grip that he could barely speak. In his head, he screamed for Garret to touch him, suck him.

"I will, Holden. I will. I want you more than I've ever wanted anyone." Garret's words were as soft as the breath wafting over Holden's cock.

As Holden watched, Garret cupped his balls in his palm, kneading them with an expert touch. Holden groaned loudly as pleasure ripped through him. His eyes met Garret's. Slowly lowering his mouth to Holden's cock, Garret swirled his tongue over the thick head, lapping up the leaking pre-cum. Heart slamming in his chest, Holden gasped for air, as his whole body went up in flames. He sucked in a rough breath as Garret slid his mouth down over Holden's cock, taking almost all of it. Garret's fingers curled tightly around the base and his other hand gently teased Holden's balls and the crease of his ass.

The hot wet suction of Garret's mouth on his cock felt like no other blow job he'd ever gotten. Holden shivered as Garret's tongue swirled and slurped around the thick head. The tip of his tongue teased the slit and flicked over the ridge before finding the spot that sent Holden into spasms of joy.

"Holy fuck! That feels so good!" he exclaimed, his hands reaching for Garret's head.

The texture of Garret's silky hair between his fingers was a counterpoint to the heated suction on Holden's cock. He'd never had a blow job be so perfect or feel so good. Garret knew exactly how to lick, suck, stroke in a rhythm that sent Holden's senses into a realm of pleasure he never knew existed. The tight wet heat of Garret's mouth was better than any pussy he'd ever fucked and he knew without a doubt that he was going to make a total fool of himself by not lasting.

When Garret's fingers stroked over the tight bud of his anus, Holden couldn't hold back a yowl of pure masculine pleasure. His whole body went rigid, his dragon clawing at him as smoke poured from his nose. Holden's eyes met Garret's as his balls tightened painfully and he cried out, "Oh, fuck, Garret! I'm gonna come!"

Instead of backing off as so many women did when his ejaculation was imminent, Garret sucked him with renewed vigor. Again Garret stroked his anus with a finger, this time pressing against it slightly as his thumb stroked over Holden's perineum. Fire exploded inside Holden and he groaned Garret's name as he came, his cock pumping out more cum than he could ever remember spewing before.

Garret sucked and swallowed, his velvety throat muscles massaging Holden's cock as it jerked and twitched in his mouth. The sensation in his cock and body was far beyond any Holden had ever experienced. Sweat shone on his skin, and his breathing was rapid and uneven. His muscles felt weak, and his whole body trembled in the aftermath of his orgasm.

Garret licked and sucked his way down Holden's now deflating cock. When it popped free of Garret's mouth, the green dragon licked his lips in satisfaction.

"C'mere," Holden rasped, feeling weak and barely able to speak.

Garret knelt on the side of the bed beside Holden, his hard cock jerking. Its head dripped pre-cum. Holden reached up and pulled Garret down on top of him, his mouth seeking his mate's. The feel of Garret's hard aroused body rubbing against his as they kissed made Holden aware of how far he had actually come in his acceptance of Garret. The feel of Garret's cock rubbing against his naked thigh, the taste of his own cum in Garret's mouth as they sucked each other's tongues sent lust racing through him again even though he'd just come.

"Garret, I can't... I'm not ready to..." he stammered against Garret's mouth, trying to tell him that he wanted to help him come, but he wasn't ready to do what Garret had done to him. Just the thought of licking and sucking Garret's cock aroused him, but fear held him in a steely grasp. He'd never done anything like that before, had never even thought about it, and thinking about it now terrified him.

"Sssh." Garret raised his head and smiled. Holden melted inside. When Garret smiled, the sun came out from behind a cloud.

Garret's hands stroked over Holden's body. "I know you're not ready. I can feel you trembling because I'm lying on you and touching you. This is all way too new."

The longer Garret lay on him, the more Holden began to relax even though he could feel his lover's thick cock throbbing with arousal. He raised his hands and stroked them over Garret's shoulders and back, touching the clan mark in the small of his back. His mate sucked in a harsh breath and his cock jumped.

"You like that," Holden murmured with satisfaction, touching the clan mark again.

Garret shivered and Holden clasped his arms around Garret's hard body, stroking him more boldly now. Garret began to moan and Holden kissed him again, their tongues tangling in a dance of seduction.

"Gods, Holden. I want you so much. Just the touch of your hands on my skin is going to make me come," Garret groaned against Holden's mouth.

Holden pulled back from Garret's face slightly as an idea came to him. He smoothed his hands down over Garret's shoulders to cup his firm ass. He might not know how to make love to man, but he knew how to touch a cock. After all, he touched his own all the time. With only a slight hesitation, he reached for Garret's cock, his fingers curving around its thickness, stroking slowly, the way he liked to stroke his own cock. Garret's eyes went wide, the elongated pupils making his face seem even more lust-ridden.

"You like this? You like me touching your cock? Stroking you?" Holden murmured as he pressed his body against Garret's, his hand sweeping in long strokes over Garret's hot flesh. He could feel Garret trembling, feel the rapid rise and fall of his chest as he grew more excited.

Holden used Garret's free-flowing pre-cum to slick up his fingers so they glided easily along the thick shaft. He brushed his mouth against Garret's in short, hot kisses that matched the strokes of his hand. He knew he had to be doing it right when Garret began to pump his hips into Holden's strokes.

As Garret's rough breathing filled his ears, Holden kissed him harder, pinching his nipples as he continued squeezing and stroking his mate's cock. Garret's whole body pressed against Holden's, his hips grinding into that fist. He nipped at Garret's lower lip and their gazes met and held.

Garret let out a long low moan as his hips pumped into Holden's hand faster and faster. "Holden, I'm going to come!" he whispered roughly, his eyes wild.

Holden squeezed him harder, his fist moving in a twisting motion. "Come for me, baby. I want you to. Show me how much you want me," he said, feeling his heart race as Garret made a rumbling sound in the back of his throat. Every sound and movement Garret made turned him on. He felt like his skin was on fire.

Garret went rigid as Holden kissed him quickly then sucked at the side of his neck. "Oh, gods, I'm coming!" The thick cock in Holden's hand jerked powerfully and he felt the hot splash of Garret's cum against his lower abdomen. Garret shuddered, clutching at Holden's back with his hands, burying his face in his lover's shoulder.

"Oh, gods, Holden, I love you!"

The sound of Garret's words echoed in the bedroom. He shuddered and shook in Holden's arms as if his physical and emotional release had drained him. Holden cradled his mate against his body, stroking him soothingly and brushing light kisses against his stubbled jaw. As much as Garret's words scared him, Holden knew they were the truth. The man had fallen in love with him. He knew that he felt something very deep and profound for Garret but he wasn't sure he could call it love. At least, not yet anyway.

Holden nudged Garret over on the bed and they sat up, watching each other speculatively. Garret's eyes seemed almost wounded by his confession. In an effort to ease him, Holden touched the sticky cum on his body, raising a finger to his mouth and tasting Garret's essence. Garret's eyes darkened.

"I don't want to hurt you, Garret. I'm going to try my damnedest not to, but I can't say those words just yet, just like I'm not ready to suck your cock or let you fuck me," Holden told his lover in a low, worried voice. "I need some time to get used to this. I want you. The gods know how much I want you and after what just happened between us, you should know it too. But it's new for me. And it's scary."

Garret leaned into Holden's body and kissed him lightly on the mouth. "I know. I'm sorry. I didn't mean to put that pressure on you. I went crazy when you touched me."

Holden smiled. "I liked it. So far, I've liked everything we've done. But now, can we eat our cold dinner? I need some meat to jump start my metabolism and maybe then we can take another stab at this before we go to bed."

"We?" Garret's eyes looked at him questioningly.

Holden nodded and stood up, reaching to grab a handful of tissues from the bedside table. As he wiped cum off himself, he said, "Yeah. You're my mate. And after the way you just sucked my cock, do you think I'd let you sleep in the other room?"

That brilliant smile flashed out again and Garret stood up. "Shall we eat the cold food or order more?" he asked, happiness lighting his expressive face.

Holden's heart turned over in his chest and he realized that he'd never felt quite this happy after sex before. "We'll order more, and we can eat the cold food while we wait. I think I saw a microwave if we need it. We're dragons. The more meat the better. Fuel us and we can fuck all night," he joked.

"Promise?" Garret growled.

"Let's eat and then I'll show you that I don't say anything I don't mean," Holden told his mate, leaning over to give him a quick hard kiss.

Chapter Six

Heaven had nothing on Holden Antaeus. The man had completely sent him round the bend with lust and then satisfied it with the simple touch of his hand. Well, perhaps simple wasn't exactly the right word. What had happened between them in Holden's bedroom was complicated by emotions and mating bonds, confusion and fear. And not all of those things were on Holden's side. Garret had a full compliment of confusion and fear too. They just happened to be about different things.

Dressed only in their jeans, shirtless, barefoot, and commando, they wolfed down their cold prime rib as they waited for fresh steaks to arrive from room service. Garret tried not to think about what would happen after they ate. Anticipation held him in a relentless grip that threatened to turn him into a babbling idiot at any moment. Somehow, he managed to keep himself together and focused on the information Holden gave him about the company.

Talking about Antaeus International was safe and innocuous. Except when Holden spoke, Garret found himself staring at the man's mouth, reliving how it tasted and what it felt like. Unfortunately, his wandering thoughts seeped out no matter how hard he tried to contain them. Even though Holden's demeanor remained the same, when room service knocked on the door, he shot out of his chair like a bullet from a gun.

Garret's appetite waned a little. He really didn't want to frighten Holden off. Keeping himself under control was imperative. Holden's nervousness had to be overcome with patience and understanding. After all, in the space of a day, he'd literally left one life behind for a new one. A life that included a mate and sex with a man. Two things no straight man would be ready for so soon.

If there had been a way for Garret to get a better sense of where Holden's head was at, he would have felt a lot better about the situation. As it stood, trying to peek into the man's head when he was shielding hard against it would be an invasion of privacy and Garret couldn't risk the loss of trust that would occur if he tried. So he sat there at the dinner table, watching the room service waiters load the dirty dishes on a cart and set out the new plates of steaming food, all the while speculating on just what thoughts tumbled around in Holden's head.

When the waiters left, Holden returned to his seat, holding a bottle of wine. "You could just ask, Garret," he said in a mild tone as he poured two glasses of the ruby liquid.

"The things I want to know, I doubt you'd tell me," Garret replied honestly. "It's not just about what you think. It's about what you feel."

Holden nodded. "Forty eight hours ago I was fucking a woman and now I'm letting you suck my cock and liking it." A deep sigh escaped him. "I'm no prude, Garret. I liked what you did to me. I liked what I did to you, as non-threatening as it was. I'm not comfortable with the full range of sexual possibilities even though I've never thought of myself as a homophobe. I never thought in terms of 'them' and 'us' sexually. So I guess what it boils down to is that I need to get comfortable with *you*, with the fact that you're my mate, with the fact that I'll be having sex with a man for the rest of my life."

Garret shook his head. Holden had focused on the sexual rather than the emotional. Finding your mate was about both, but the emphasis for Garret was not sexual. He figured if they could accept each other as mates, everything else would fall into place. Holden kept bringing it all back to sex, which told Garret that Holden's insecurities were all related to sex with a man. A light bulb came on for Garret. He figured that somehow Holden thought that if he were to accept Garret fully as his mate and begin reciprocating sexually, it meant he was gay. What it all meant to Garret was that his mate had some very narrow ideas about sexual attraction, gender, and mating.

Reaching for his knife and fork he said, "You need to get comfortable with me as your mate, Holden. The rest will fall into place once you've truly accepted that and begun to feel something for me. It's falling into place for me much quicker than it is for you because I'm open to having a man as my mate and my lover. "

Anger flashed in Holden's amber eyes. "I'm not closed-minded."

"No, I can tell that you are working very hard to bring yourself to a better level of acceptance. But you're still thinking in gender specific terms, Holden. I'm not, therefore my acceptance of you as my mate is unconditional." Garret paused, his eyes meeting Holden's. Anger and confusion warred on his mate's face.

Gesturing toward Holden's plate with his fork he said, "Let's not waste another meal. We can argue semantics afterward."

Holden looked down at his plate and picked up his fork and knife. "It's not semantics if it's how you feel," he growled.

"I can go back to my room after dinner, Holden. You don't have to be with me anymore tonight." Garret pointed out the obvious, his curiosity about Holden's thoughts and feelings rising sharply. "You've come a long way toward acceptance and I love you all the more for it. You just need to understand that the emotional bonds are winding around me more tightly as each hour passes. It's difficult for me to be near you and not tell you how I feel."

The knife and fork clattered to Holden's plate and he grasped his wine glass drinking deeply from it. He set it down and his eyes speared Garret to his chair. "I'm not a child, Garret. I can handle you telling me about your feelings. Just don't expect me to reciprocate before I'm ready. Just so you know, I feel the emotional bonds building too. However, I analyze data for a living. I want to know that I've built an emotional foundation with you based on how we interact with each other not on the mating mechanisms in our DNA."

Caught by surprise, Garret stared wide eyed at Holden. "You want to learn to love me aside from the natural urges to mate."

Holden's dark head dipped in acquiescence. He picked up his utensils again. Cutting into his steak he said, "I would want the same if my mate was a woman."

Garret's emotions churned within him. At every turn, Holden Antaeus surprised him. Sure, the man probably did have some hang ups about being gay and about sex with men; it was early and his feelings were bound to change. However, his take on mating and feelings outside of the relentless pull of mating bonds were not something Garret could ignore.

They finished their meal in near silence and piled the dishes on the cart, setting it out in the hotel corridor to be picked up later. The instant the door shut, Garret tensed.

"Maybe it would be easier if I went to my own room," he said in a low tone, repeating his earlier offer.

Holden padded toward him, that lean tennis-hardened body like a finely coiled spring, appearing relaxed but filled with tension. Garret gritted his teeth as Holden reached out. Warm fingertips stroked over the curves of Garret's biceps. His cock filled with heat.

"I've never backed away from a challenge, Garret," Holden murmured, his eyes following the path of his fingers. "An Antaeus faced with an obstacle figures out a way over it or bulldozes it to the ground. We're not known for skirting issues."

Garret had heard a lot of things about the Antaeus family. In business, they were feared and respected, and known to be brutally honest, relentless competitors. On a personal level, Garret had already come to the conclusion that Holden lived his life the same way. The problem was that Garret didn't like being thought of as an issue to be dealt with.

"Stop thinking. There are a lot of layers to this mating thing," Holden said quietly. "The emotional layer is there. I feel it building, but it's not what's paramount inside me at the moment. Right now, you need to know that I'm looking at your mouth and my cock is starting to respond. I've never been able to resist a good blow job. And, Garret—" His hand came up and captured Garret's chin, his eyes boring into his mate's. "You gave me one of the best blow jobs I've ever had. Why the hell would I even think of turning down the possibility of another one?"

Garret's cock swelled when Holden said he was becoming aroused. Their first encounter had left him drained, yet wanting more. His need, both sexually and emotionally, for Holden grew steadily inside him. Wryly, he also realized that his own competitive nature picked up on Holden's word choices. "One of the best blow jobs" wasn't good enough for Garret. He would make the man forget anyone else had ever sucked his cock.

Holden grinned openly, his firm lips parting to show even white teeth. Garret's gut clenched as the desire to kiss his mate and thrust his tongue into the heated depths of Holden's mouth caused his cock to harden almost painfully. Taking a step forward, Holden's body brushed Garret's. Pleasure shot through him with white hot intensity. Every nerve ending, every atom in his body responded to the proximity of Holden's body. Inside, his dragon paced, eager to be mated, eager to taste the pleasure only Holden could provide. Smoke drifted from his nostrils as the crisp lime scent that Holden gave off grew stronger. The increase in scent indicated Holden's arousal.

Never had Garret been the type to take his sexual cues from others. He was Alpha, used to being the one who initiated, who led. Having to restrain himself, to let Holden dictate the pace, had his dragon growling with impatience and his arousal quickly built to wildfire proportions within him.

Holden let go of Garret's chin, his hands skating over the hard planes of his mate's shoulders. Garret shuddered as pleasure washed over him, causing his skin to ripple, the faint tracing of his green scales becoming visible. He fought his dragon, who wanted the shift. Now, was not the time or the place. His tail alone would take out the dining table and the sofa, he thought ruefully.

The grin on Holden's mouth widened and Garret knew his mate had heard his thoughts. With a growl, he wrapped his arms around Holden. The other man stiffened slightly then shivered as Garret's fingers found the lines that swirled down Holden's spine.

"Your touch on my clan mark does something to my body I've never felt before," Holden panted, his chest heaving as a fine tremor went through him.

Garret realized that he was becoming tuned to the reactions of Holden's body. The sense of right that filled him when he touched

Holden grew with each passing minute, every stroke of his fingers over the muscle, sinew, and bone that was his new mate. Their gazes met and held. Garret eased back the control on his thoughts, letting Holden see just what he desired. With a groan, Holden tilted his head and pressed his mouth to Garret's.

Sucking on Holden's tongue, feeling the press of his mate's growing erection against his own groin through the layers of their jeans, Garret knew what he wanted. He knew how he wanted this night of exploration and discovery to end. He wanted Holden to take him, to mark him, and bind them together.

Tearing his mouth from Garret's, Holden shook his head. "No mating. Not yet. It's too soon," he panted, smoking trailing from his nostrils. "But the other thing you want, to be taken...*fucked*...I think I can accommodate that."

Garret sucked in a breath. "Lube. We need lube." His mind fuzzy with the lust that had taken over his body, Garret tried to remember if he'd brought some.

"Get it." Holden's command was delivered with a gleam in his golden eyes that made Garret quiver with anticipation.

As Holden turned away toward his bedroom, Garret rushed to his own room, his shaking hands tearing at the toiletries kit on the bathroom counter. "Shit, shit!" he muttered, raking through the items in the case.

His fingers closed on a new tube of lubricant and his cock twitched, pressing painfully against the zipper of his jeans. Gods, he needed to get a grip. If he didn't, he'd be spilling the instant Holden thrust that beautiful cock inside him. He shivered. He now knew what Holden's cock looked like, tasted like and felt like. Letting Holden fuck him was the ultimate submission to his mate. Despite having been fucked before, he'd never relinquished control in a sexual situation. Yet, he was perfectly willing to hand over the lock and key to his mind, body, heart...and ass...to Holden.

On slightly rubbery legs, Garret walked across the main room of the suite to Holden's bedroom. As he stepped inside, his heart slammed painfully against his ribs. The naked, sculpted planes of Holden's body were completely on display as he leaned over, stripping back the covers of the bed. Then he sprawled on the sheet, rolling over so that Garret could see his straining erection.

Garret licked his suddenly dry lips and Holden grinned. Reaching down, he began to stroke his cock with slow seductive movements, making Garret wish he was the hand.

"You're staring at me like you think I'm dessert," Holden chuckled.

"Not you. *That.*" Garret gestured toward Holden's cock with his chin. He tossed the lube onto the mattress, ripped his jeans off, and crawled onto the bed, taking Holden's erection from his hand and sliding his mouth down over the hard flesh, deep throating him.

Holden groaned loudly, his hands coming up to cup Garret's head. His hips thrust upward, pressing more of his cock into Garret's throat. Heat spiraled through Garret as he sucked greedily on Holden's cock. The hard flesh tasted salty and smelled of arousal and the tartness of Holden's lime scent. Garret had the quick thought that sucking Holden was like doing tequila shots...lime, salt, and a burst of alcohol that burned its way down before going straight to your head. The thought dissipated as he concentrated on sucking Holden. He teased the hard flesh, his cheeks hollowing as he sucked and licked, his throat muscles working in concert with his lips and tongue to drive his mate insane with lust.

As Garret's hands stroked Holden's taut balls, he opened his thoughts to his lover.

Gods, Holden. I love how you taste. I love the feel of you in my mouth, and the sound of your moans. Your pleasure is my pleasure.

Holden moaned again and writhed beneath Garret's mouth and hands. Garret thought his own cock would explode as he sucked Holden, putting every ounce of technique he knew into pleasuring his lover. His fingers brushed the crease of Holden's ass, stroking inward to flick across the puckered bud of his anus. A tremor went through Holden so strongly that Garret felt it ripple the muscles beneath his fingertips. Then Holden's hands slowly forced Garret off his cock. As the thick head slipped from his mouth, he stared quizzically at Holden.

"I'm not coming in your mouth this time. This time, I'm fucking you," Holden said, his breath coming in harsh pants. "When I come this time, I want to be deep inside your hot ass."

Desire so fierce it made him tremble, seized Garret in a rough hand. He reached for the lube, handing it to Holden. He nudged his lover aside and sprawled face down on the sheets, pressing his ass into the air as he braced his knees on the mattress. He felt rather than saw Holden kneel behind him, heard him suck in a breath and knew his mate was staring at his ass.

Holden blew a stream of air onto Garret's ass and balls. He felt himself tighten involuntarily at the sensuous contact, his anus contracted, his balls pulling up close to his body. Holden's hand stroked Garret's tight sac, kneading gently for a moment. Then Garret felt the wet heat of the lube that Holden had obviously warmed in his hand. Holden's blunt fingers rubbed the lube onto his anus. As the sphincter loosened, one finger pressed inward.

Garret pressed his hips back against the invading digit. The lube made the insertion easy and he felt Holden squirt more lube on his anus as the long finger probed deep within him. Hot friction radiated out from Garret's tender hole as Holden began to finger-fuck him. Garret bit back the urge to hurry Holden along as sensation began to build in his body. He sucked in a breath, letting it out slowly as Holden inserted a second finger in his ass. The slight burn disappeared in seconds.

Just like before, the silence of the room was punctuated by the sound of their harsh breathing and low moans. Garret shivered as Holden's fingers slid from his ass, but before he could protest, he felt something pressing relentlessly against his anus. Breathing out in shallow pants, Garret felt his ass open to take Holden's thick cock. His hole burned as Holden pressed more firmly, inching more of his cock into Garret's ass. Cool wetness burst against his flesh as Holden squirted even more lube onto the place where they were joined. With a grunt, Holden pressed in further.

Garret pushed back and the thick length of Holden's cock slid all the way home, his balls slapping up against Garret's. With a whimper as sensation took over his groin front to back, Garret felt his cock growing impossibly harder.

Geez, Garret. You're so fucking tight and hot. I've never fucked anyone this hot before.

Holden's hands settled on Garret's hips, using them for leverage as he pulled back slightly. Pleasure shot through Garret's body as Holden's cock head pressed against his prostate. A loud moan escaped him and his hand fumbled for his cock. Desire flooded him to the point where all he could think of was the exquisite feel of Holden's cock filling him, pressing that pleasure center inside his hot passage, and stroking his cock so that he could come with his lover.

As Holden's hips set up a rhythm of short strokes that made Garret feel every inch of his thick cock, they both let go of the control they'd clung to earlier, no longer speaking out loud at all. Every stroke of Holden's cock made Garret shiver and he tried to keep his balance while stroking his own cock. Holden's tongue licked along Garret's spine making him groan loudly. The heat and friction in his ass grew, becoming more and more pleasurable as the minutes passed.

Holden snaked one arm around Garret's abdomen, pulling him up onto his knees. With his back cradled against Holden's chest, the black dragon's hard pelvis rubbed against Garret's clan mark. Shaking, Garret turned his head and Holden's mouth slashed down onto his. The kiss was hard and desperate, each of them seeking the ultimate pleasure from each other's bodies. Holden slid his hand down Garret's belly, reaching to replace Garret's hand with his own. At the feel of Holden's hand on his cock, Garret broke the kiss, coming down on all fours. Holden bent over him, fucking his ass hard while stroking his thick erection.

Gods, Holden! Your cock is driving me insane. Every stroke fills me with pleasure. Can't you feel what you do to me?

Holden grunted, his fingers twisting over Garret's cock. *I want you. I want to fuck you so hard and so good and fill you so full of my cum you won't ever want another cock in your ass.*

No, Holden! Only you. By the gods, only you can make me feel like this. I've never wanted anyone this much. I'll never want anyone else again.

Rough pants filled Garret's ears as Holden fucked him harder than he'd ever been fucked before. He wondered briefly if he'd be sore in the morning since Holden also had the biggest cock he'd ever taken, but the thought passed out of his head quickly because he just didn't care. He belonged to Holden and the man could do whatever he wanted to Garret.

Holden's sweat dripped onto his back and shoulders as Garret began to feel lightheaded from the constant stimulation of his prostate and cock. His skin tingled when Holden scraped his curved dragon fangs over Garret's shoulders.

Mate me. Please, Holden!

Not yet, Holden's thoughts were grim as he openly fought to keep control. *Soon, but not yet. First, you need to come for me. Do you like my hand on your cock? Do you like how my cock fills your ass? How it knows that it is home? Your ass is mine forever, Garret. It belongs to my cock.*

Holden's possessive, raunchy thoughts coupled with the twisting strokes of his hand on Garret's cock and the relentless thrust of his thick erection into Garret's ass caused the green dragon to quickly hit the point of no return. With a loud cry, he erupted into orgasm, his cock jerking in Holden's hand. His hot seed shot out onto the mattress and down over his lover's stroking fingers. He shuddered and shook, his body convulsing, his ass clamping down convulsively on Holden's pistoning cock.

Holy fuck, Garret, your ass is squeezing me! I'm coming!

"Garret!"

Holden's yell reverberated through the room and through Garret's mind. The emotion-filled, shocked amazement of Holden's intense pleasure slammed into his head at the same time that he felt the physical heat of his lover's cum pouring into his ass. They both shook from the force of orgasms stronger than any they'd ever experienced. When it was over, when the tremors had died down and they breathed normally again,

Garret felt Holden's cock slip wetly from his ass as his mate released Garret's now limp member. He shook from being on his hands and knees through such rough sex, but he wouldn't move for all the gold in Fort Knox.

Garret drew a shuddering breath as Holden nuzzled the back of his neck. *Shower. We need a shower now.*

Holden, I don't think I can stand and besides, there's the wet spot to deal with...

I'll carry you. Holden kissed the point of Garret's shoulder and trailed languid kisses and caresses all along his arms. He licked the spot beneath Garret's ear causing him to shiver. He'd never known that was an erogenous zone.

Yeah, right. Garret chuckled out loud at the picture in Holden's mind of Garret slung over his shoulder in a fireman's carry. *You like that image because my ass is in the air.*

And your cock is rubbing against me. Holden's amusement turned to a mental grimace. *Arggh. Wet spot. Shit.*

Somehow they supported each other's wobbly sex-weakened steps into the bathroom. They dealt with the wet spot then got in the shower where they leaned on each other tiredly. Minds fuzzy in the aftermath of their orgasms, washing each other lazily, they used the time to learn more about each other's bodies. To Garret's acute embarrassment, Holden wanted to ensure he hadn't hurt his new mate. He wanted to clean Garret's ass and inspect it for injury, something Garret wasn't about to allow.

I don't think so, Holden. I can do it myself.

Holden kissed him roughly, shoving him back against the tile wall. *I want to do it. I want to know that you can take all of me, that I haven't hurt you and this is going to work.*

Garret pushed at his mate, asserting himself. *Damn you. I'm not your fucking girlfriend, Holden. I've had sex with men before. Maybe not as big as you, but I know what I can handle and what I can't. There's no need to coddle me like I'm some weak female.*

Holden's dark brows shot up in surprise. *I'm sorry. I didn't mean it the way you think.*

Roughly, Garret took the soap from Holden, washing himself quickly and efficiently while his lover stood in the shower spray watching with hooded eyes. When he was done, he shoved the soap back at Holden and stepped out of the shower, reaching for a towel.

"I'll be in the other room. I need a drink."

With a towel wrapped around his hips and water still running down his torso, Garret retreated to the main room of the suite, heading straight for the wet bar. He poured himself two fingers of whiskey and downed them. Then he poured another.

Walking over to the glass slider, he stared out at the darkness. In the past, in every sexual situation, he had always been in control. But his emotions ran deep at the moment and his fear that Holden would never be able to accept him had made him afraid to assert himself for fear of losing his mate. Because of his fear, he'd allowed Holden to dictate their sexual encounters thus far. But that wasn't who he was. He wanted a partner. An equal.

"We seem to constantly be apologizing to one another."

Garret turned to find Holden standing a few feet from him in a hotel robe. He raised one brow at his lover and finished his drink, setting the glass on a table by the couch. Holden shifted uncomfortably. Two spots of color burned on his cheekbones.

"I'm sorry I treated you like that. You're not a woman. You're a man. An Alpha. I had no right to try to turn you into my pet or something," he said awkwardly.

Garret drew a deep breath and took a couple of steps toward his mate, stopping a few feet away. "Holden, you need to understand that if I've taken a submissive role with you, it's because I've been afraid to scare you, to lose you. I would do almost anything to ensure that doesn't happen, but I'm not submissive. With you, I want to be equal."

He didn't know if what he was about to say would ruin his chances with Holden, but in his gut, Garret knew it was time for Holden to know who and what he was. "I'm not your bitch, a vessel for you to fuck," he said in a low voice, his words quiet and emphatic. "I am your mate, your partner. And even though I loved every minute of your big cock in my ass, I have to tell you that I *burn* to fuck you. I want to feel your body beneath mine, feel my cock hot in your ass as you take all of me and love it."

Holden's eyes widened, but he didn't back away and Garret didn't feel any revulsion coming off him either. "I understand," he replied, evenly. "I should have known. You're no Omega begging to be taken."

Garret laughed then. "Oh, I'll beg you to take me, but I'll want my turn too." He took another step forward then reached out to wrap his hand around the back of Holden's neck, drawing him closer. "One day, when this relationship has gelled, we'll share a woman too, because the gods know I love pussy just as much as you do."

Now, it was Holden's turn to arch one brow up. "That would be cheating on your mate," he teased.

"Not if we do it together." Garret's words came out in a whisper as he took Holden's mouth in a hot, hard kiss, their lips mashing together, tongues tangling roughly.

When Holden's hands jerked the damp towel from his body, Garret pushed open the lapels of the hotel robe and their naked bodies cleaved together. Breaking the kiss, Garret pressed damp kisses to the strong column of Holden's throat. "We need to go back to bed," he muttered.

Grabbing Garret's hands, Holden pulled them away from his body, shaking his head. "Sean has plans for us tomorrow, remember? Any more sex tonight and we won't be able to handle what he throws at us."

"Shall I go back to my room then?" Garret teased.

"Fuck no." Holden's hand caressed Garret's rising cock. "You're coming to bed with me."

"Ahhh." Garret smiled at his mate, and let his hands trail down the ridges of Holden's abdomen to his cock. "Okay. That works for me. You haven't fully appreciated the beauty of grindage yet anyway."

"Grindage?" Holden looked a little startled as Garret took him by the hand and led him back to the bedroom.

"Yes. It's just like prom night except that you do it naked and you get to come."

"Intriguing," Holden said with a grin as he followed Garret into the bedroom and shut the door.

Chapter Seven

Holden had never liked sleeping with anyone. Occasionally, he'd tolerate it on a trip with a girlfriend when he knew he'd spend most of the time fucking anyway. Sharing his bed and having to do the cuddling thing was the price he paid for getting his rocks off. He'd never been unwilling to pay; he just had never enjoyed it.

After Garret had shown him how exciting the grindage could really be, and after they'd cleaned up for what seemed like the umpteenth time that night, they'd settled into Holden's bed to sleep. Holden had lain stiffly on his side, knowing he would probably toss and turn and disturb Garret to the point that the man would retreat to his own room. Why he'd invited Garret to sleep with him in the first place was a mystery. He just felt compelled to do so even knowing how much he hated company when he slept.

Still, when Garret crawled into bed, smelling of his own spearmint scent and some citrus mouthwash, he had nestled his back into Holden's chest spoon fashion and fallen right asleep. Holden wriggled trying to get comfortable. He pressed his hips into Garret's ass, remembering what it had felt like to fuck the man. A wave of emotion had come over him and he'd slipped one arm around Garret, sliding the other beneath the pillows. He'd relaxed, his hand absently stroking Garret's hard abs.

The next thing he knew sun spilled into the room as he lay flat on his back with Garret's arm across his chest, one leg between his, and his face buried in Holden's shoulder. The feel of Garret's knee pressing his swelling cock had been beyond exciting. Finding that they were sharing a pillow and had apparently been cuddled together all night was disconcerting. With conflicting emotions abounding, Holden had just slid out from under Garret and gotten up.

When they reached the private dining room, Emily again snatched up Garret as if he was a lifeline. Holden found himself seated across the table from his mate and beside his brother Declan. Before Declan and Holden could do more than wish each other good morning, Sean arrived with Vahid and began passing out sheets of paper. Holden stared at his in disbelief, not hearing a word his oldest brother said.

Sean's plans for the second day of the retreat annoyed him. He might be an athlete, but he wasn't a fan of nature walks and such. Sean had planned a morning hike for everyone, putting people in groups of two, three, or four. Considering some of the odd groups Sean put together, Holden expected to be in a different group than Garret, but Sean had put them together with no one else. The only other group of two was Vahid and Emily, who tried not to look mutinous and failed.

Seated in the private dining room, as waiters served breakfast following Sean's announcement of the morning's activities, Holden stole a glance at his brother Declan. "Why the hell do you and Sean get to sit this out while I have to participate?" he bitched.

Declan shook out his napkin with a shrug. "Australia is being a prick and a half. That's my excuse. I don't know what Sean's is other than the fact that *he's* a prick and a half who likes to pull everyone else's chain," his brother replied coolly. "Why don't you wanna go hiking with Wonderboy?"

Holden gritted his teeth, counted to ten, and reminded himself that this was his older brother. The one he liked, not the one who annoyed the fuck out of him. Although Declan was doing a damned good job of pissing him off just like Sean. "His name is Garret," Holden growled in a low voice, his eyes darting across the table at Garret who sat with a glowering Emily.

His brother looked up from his Eggs Florentine, surprise in the depths of his golden eyes. "You know, Holden, I called him that yesterday and you didn't flinch, but you did smirk, as if you knew something I didn't know," Declan pointed out with cool logic. "Today, you're getting pissy with me because I didn't use our newest executive's proper name. What the hell gives?"

Lying to Declan never worked. Every time he had in the past, he'd gotten caught and Declan had made him pay in some way. At the same time, he wasn't ready to tell Declan the truth and certainly not at the breakfast table with every executive from Antaeus International within earshot. He could just see the wide eyed shocked faces and hear the whispers.

"Did he just say he fucked the new finance guy last night?"

"That's one way to get ahead, give the boss head!"

Holden blinked rapidly, trying to clear the vision from his head. Across the table, Garret's lips twitched as he tried to suppress a grin. Sharing thoughts could be damned inconvenient at times. And what the hell could he say to Declan that wouldn't be a lie?

Just tell him you like the way I play tennis. He doesn't have to know what kind of balls and rackets you're thinking about.

Eyes narrowed, Holden glared at Garret across the table. *It doesn't work with balls and rackets. The euphemism is supposed to be baseball, balls and bats.*

Garret cut into his omelet and offered Holden a glimpse of that smile that always did him in. *Just mention the tennis. He'll pass everything over for now. But eventually, Holden, your family needs to know.*

Holden raised a sardonic brow. *Believe me; no one knows that more than I do.* He glanced over at Declan again. "I'm just pissed about the damn hiking. I hate fucking hiking."

Declan gave him a sour look. "Take a towel with you. There are hot springs up the trail Sean's assigned you. You can go skinny dipping and relax. Nothing like a soak in the hot spring to ease dragon tension. The water's so hot you'll think you let your dragonfire escape," he said in a droll voice.

"Are you nuts? I'm not getting naked when Emily and Vahid could show up any second." Yeah, getting naked around Garret when any of their colleagues could discover them wasn't Holden's idea of a fun morning.

"Don't you ever pay attention?" Declan asked in an annoyed tone. "You and Garret are the only ones on that trail. Everyone else was assigned a trail on the other side of the lodge. Sean must really want you to bond with this guy."

Holden's hand jerked, spilling his coffee a little. Declan hadn't meant the term *bond* in an intimate way, but Holden's head processed it that way, giving him visions of himself grasping Garret's taut buttocks as he fucked him. He glanced across the table at Garret again. He was turned toward Emily, intent on whatever she was whispering in his ear.

She's complaining about Vahid. I'm not paying so much attention to her that I don't know what you were thinking. It's a good thing I don't have to get up from this table right now or everyone would see what I think of your thoughts.

The stiffness in his own groin told Holden he couldn't have risen at that moment either. He needed to learn to focus and not get so damned aroused by the least little thing that had to do with Garret. Blocking out Garret's thoughts and shielding his own from his mate, Holden listened as Declan filled him in on the newest problems with the Australian takeover.

After breakfast, Holden and Garret and their trail map went up to their suite to change. Jeans, t-shirt, hoodie, and beat up sneakers seemed good enough to Holden for a morning spent walking. He grabbed a small backpack, shoved a few things in it, including the lube, and went to the wet bar to grab some water bottles.

When Garret came in, Holden had to admit he was a little impressed. The man had on jeans and a red polo shirt, a windbreaker with reflective strips on the arms, and well worn expensive hiking boots. Apparently, hiking agreed with Garret Renquist.

"Is there a first aid kit in that backpack?" he joked, taking out more water for Garret.

His mate's brows rose. "Of course."

"Well, if something happens, you're in charge. I'm way out of my element in the woods. Torts and trees are two entirely different things."

"I am perfectly capable of taking care of you in this type of environment should something untoward occur," Garret said as his placed several bottles of water in his backpack.

Holden shot him an odd look. "Suddenly, you totally sound like a stuffed-shirt Englishman."

Garret grinned. "I am a stuffed-shirt Englishman."

"You're a bean counter too," Holden said on a chuckle as he held the door open.

Striding through to the corridor, Garret reached out and slapped Holden's ass as he went by. "I am not a bean counter."

"Are too."

"Am not."

They started down the hotel corridor, both of them grinning at their word play. Holden couldn't remember the last time he'd had such simple fun with someone. Unfortunately, his good humor didn't last. Hiking really wasn't his milieu. The outdoors, other than a tennis court or the beach, wasn't really his thing either. Trees and dirt and nature always defeated him in some way.

On this day, he discovered the trail was steeper and more difficult than he expected. The backs of his legs pulled uncomfortably and his annoyance grew. He didn't want his new mate to see him out of sorts over such a stupid thing, but he'd just had it with the nature stuff. His tolerance for nature went only so far.

Halfway up the mountain, Holden hit his threshold. He stopped and plopped down on a boulder, eyeing Garret with a frown. "I'm not a fucking nature boy. This sucks."

Garret stared at him wide eyed and Holden realized that his mate had figured out he wasn't going any further. His stomach rolled as he wondered if copping out and quitting would make his mate look at him with disgust.

~***~

Garret drew a deep breath of the pine scented air. He could tell that Holden's thoughts were in a bit of turmoil and wondered what had set him off this time. "It's nice out here today. And the hike hasn't been difficult at all. I don't understand what you think is so hard."

"It's not hard. But I'm a city boy. I'm not into all this nature crap." Holden scowled, reaching for the bottle of water that hung from his backpack.

As he drank, Garret looked around the trail. It was wide here and a few yards further he could see that the trail branched. He thought he saw a puff of smoke down the right side trail and frowned, hoping no one was smoking. When he saw another plume drifting upward he wondered if one of the other dragons was on this trail although Sean had said that no one else had been given this route.

He drew in another deep breath and the scent of sulfur reached him. He turned to Holden with a grin. "Hey, we've found it!"

"Found what?" his mate said in a grumpy voice.

"The hot springs Declan mentioned." Garret pointed toward the puffs of steam that he'd mistaken for smoke.

"Really?" Holden was on his feet and looking in the direction of the hot springs. He sniffed the air and a grin broke out across his face. "Fuck, yeah. Let's go!"

Pleased that Holden's bad mood seemed to have lifted now that they'd found the hot springs, Garret led the way down the trail, following the tell tale steam. Leaving the trail, they made their way through a thick stand of pines and emerged in a secluded, lush, green clearing. Holden strode into the middle of the glade and set his backpack down.

"It's very green," Garret said looking around. "I thought there was a drought or something."

"Bah. Never listen to the news. They dramatize everything," Holden muttered as he struggled with his clothes.

Garret frowned as Holden's hoodie hit the ground beside his backpack. Next came his t-shirt. "What are you doing?" he asked, striding across the glade toward Holden.

His mate looked up, golden eyes brimming with laughter, the pupils elongated. "Getting naked." Holden popped the buttons on his jeans and moments later his shoes and socks, jeans and boxer briefs were on the grass.

A sigh of satisfaction escaped Garret as he watched Holden stretch his arms toward the sky. The man had the most perfect body Garret had ever seen. He felt his cock stir behind his zipper. Smoke poured from Holden's nostrils, wreathing his head in a growing cloud and Garret realized what was about to happen.

Golden, confetti like shimmers filled the air where Holden stood. Within moments, instead of the hot, naked body of his mate, a huge black dragon appeared before Garret. The dragon let out a loud roar, its curved fangs slashing the air as the roar made the pines tremble.

"Show off," Garret said with a grin.

I heard that, asshole.

Garret stared up at Holden's big black scaled head questioningly. The amber eyes gleamed at him.

What? You didn't think you could hear me? You're my mate, no one else can hear me so well when I am in this form. Besides, I can't shield you when I'm in dragon form. If I do, I can't communicate with you.

"That's true." Garret set his backpack down beside Holden's.

Get naked.

Holden's thought had a sly emphasis and Garret stared up at him incredulously. "What? You want me to get naked?"

Holden's big dragon head bobbed.

"Why?" Garret asked and Holden slapped his tail against the ground. The earth rumbled beneath Garret's feet and his eyes widened. "Oh, fuck. You have to be joking."

Holden shook his big head.

So not joking. And if you don't get naked and shift, the next time I catch you in shifted form, I'll pin you down and fuck your ass raw.

Startled, Garret looked into Holden's huge golden eyes. There was laughter there but Garret got the sense that Holden wasn't quite lying about the fucking either. As a threat, it wasn't much of a deterrent, Garret thought, his mind flashing back to the night before. Being fucked by Holden had some distinct advantages. Garret pulled off his windbreaker and shirt. It took only a few moments to get down to his skin. Holden's eyes never left him.

Fuck, you're beautiful.

Garret grimaced at Holden's thoughts. Men weren't beautiful. He certainly wasn't beautiful.

Shut up and shift already! And if I say you're good looking, you are. I have great taste.

A chuckle escaped Garret as he concentrated on the shift. Golden sparkles shimmered in the air around him and he felt his dragon stretch, embracing the shift. When his form took shape, Garret knew exactly what Holden saw. A green dragon, slightly longer than Holden's form, but not as bulky, his tail spiked and deadly, the iridescent shimmer of his wings stretching up toward the sky with a wingspan greater than that of Holden's wings. His serpentine head swiveled toward Holden.

Geez, Garret. You coulda warned me. Tinged with amusement and admiration, Holden's thoughts entered Garret's head easily even in dragon form.

Warned you about what? Garret folded his wings and took a couple of steps toward Holden, stopping when their chests were but a few feet apart.

Holden snorted, smoke blowing out of his nostrils in a big puff. *That you had a spiked tail. I was gonna offer to hold tails with you.*

Garret could see the teasing in Holden's eyes, but at the same time, he felt the swell of emotion that rose in his mate. It matched the emotion inside him that threatened to overwhelm his senses. Holding tails was an act of dragon intimacy, like holding hands. However, while someone might hold the hand of a friend, dragons never held the tail of other dragons unless it was their mate or their parent. Even siblings never grasped tails.

Holden, I...

Garret broke off his thought and looked away. He felt too much to be able to articulate his emotions to Holden. Just in the short time they'd known each other, he'd come to understand just who Holden Antaeus was. Everything about the man screamed fairness and integrity. That alone drew Garret like a moth to a flame. All his life, he'd been surrounded by people who used one another, who used him. As a consequence, he'd chosen his lovers carefully, nice, easy-going, milquetoast individuals that he could be friends with before and after sex. Nothing in his life had prepared him for a lover like Holden. Nothing had prepared him for falling fangs over tail in love.

Turning away from Holden, Garret stared in the direction of the hot springs. Had he been in human form, his eyes would have been burning from holding back tears of emotion. Looking at Holden made him feel triumphant, yet weak as a kitten. No one had ever made him feel so vulnerable. Fear rose within him as he realized how integral Holden was to his future and his happiness. Even without the mating bonds pulling at them, Garret knew he would have fallen in love with Holden. He needed Holden to make him laugh, to make him relax, to make him trust again.

He might be an opened minded individual, but he had kept his heart and his emotions carefully guarded for nearly a century.

Something hit his shoulder hard. Caught off guard, he stumbled, his head whipping around to find Holden close by his side, preparing to butt him again with his big black head.

I don't trust many people either, Garret. Antaeus International is a family run business for a reason. My siblings and I rely on each other. For us, blood is thicker than water. So are mating bonds. Very few people get close to an Antaeus. You've earned your place with us aside from the mating bonds that you and I share.

A stream of smoke came from Holden's nostrils as he exhaled on a long breath. *When you say that you would have fallen in love with me despite the pull of the mating bonds, something responds inside me.* Arching his neck, his black scales gleaming in the afternoon sun, Holden bumped his head against Garret's in a sort of caress. At the same time, the sharp tip of his tail looped over Garret's, carefully avoiding the vicious spikes, but still managing to stroke the sensitive green scales.

A shudder went through Garret. Visions of Holden mating him in dragon form filled his head. Garret wasn't sure if they were the product of his own imagination or Holden's. Smoke billowed from his nostrils as the sexual imagery grew more detailed. His eyes met Holden's.

Garret, I think I would have fallen for you too, even without the mating bonds.

The thought was quiet and self-confident and filled with emotion. Holden bumped Garret's head again and this time, Garret responded by rubbing his head against Holden's neck. Smoke encircled their huge dragon forms as sexual tension rose within them. The urge to bend down and let Holden take him made Garret shake with lust and anticipation. He wanted to bathe Holden in his dragonfire and mate him.

Not here. We need to do it in private. And we need to know each other better before we share fire. Holden bumped his head against Garret's again, his tail still caressing Garret's spiked one. *Besides, I don't think you really want to mate in dragon form. It's really clumsy and your tail would definitely be in the way of my cock.*

Holden's eyes gleamed with amusement and the tension within Garret eased a little. He blew out a smoke ring, watching as it settled around Holden's neck then dissipated.

I wouldn't want anything to get in the way of your cock. I can't wait to feel you inside me again.

Holden snorted, his entire body shaking a little, as more smoke and a teaser of flame erupted from his nostrils. Garret knew the lack of control over his fire meant that Holden was aroused.

Aroused? Geez, Garret you have a gift for understatement, did you know that? I have a huge throbbing dragon cock at the moment and it's all your fault.

Oh really? Garret's lips curled back from his fangs in a dragon grin. His tail shifted and carefully he slid it beneath Holden's belly. Garret let the part of his tail above the spikes brush against the armor plated sheath that protected Holden's cock. At the stimulation, the huge erection slid free of the sheath, rubbing against Garret's tail.

FUCK!

Garret shivered in reaction, his own cock sliding from its sheath. He looked at Holden and found little flames erupting from his mate's nostrils with every panting breath.

Gods, Garret. You fucking turn me on and scare the piss out of me at the same time. The thought of those fucking spikes anywhere near my cock gives me the shivers. But the feel of your tail, your scales, against my erection...it's enough to make me come right now.

Garret laughed, the sound coming out as a sort of hiccupping roar. *How would we explain the bucketfuls of dragon cum to the forest rangers?*

Holden bumped his head against Garret's again. *We wouldn't. I'd make you lick it up for scaring me with those damned spikes,* he teased.

Garret thumped away from Holden. *You and what army?* He snorted and flames shot from his nostrils.

Holden's neck arched and he went into a fighting stance. Garret did the same. When Holden rushed him, Garret let his bulkier mate bounce off the armor plated scales of his chest. He swept his tail beneath Holden's feet trying to make him stumble. Holden's wings snapped out and lifted him off the ground away from Garret's spiked tail. They spent a few minutes mock fighting across the glade, tussling with each other and laughing.

Finally, Holden stretched out his wings and began to shift. The golden confetti shimmers filled the air around him until every molecule of his dragon form dissolved into the human form Garret knew best. Holden grinned up at him, hands on hips, his erection boldly arcing toward his belly button.

"Better hurry. I'm headed to the hot springs now," he said with a laugh as he gathered up his clothes and backpack.

Garret shifted, happy in the knowledge that even in dragon form, he and Holden seemed compatible. Grabbing up his things, he strode after his mate. His arousal hadn't lessened one bit and he hoped like hell that Holden had thought to bring the lube.

Someone had made the hot springs more assessable to people by placing flat stones all around the edge of the triangular shaped pool. Handholds and benches were bolted to the rock sides in the pool. Garret figured that the uneven bottom made the handholds a necessity.

Holden knelt at the side of the hot springs, his hand in the bubbling water. He glanced up as Garret dropped his clothes on the flagstones. "It's a little smelly but I bet it feels awesome," he remarked.

"Too hot for humans," Garret observed, his gaze taking in the clouds of steam that rose from the surface of the water.

Holden stood up. "I would think so. It's nearly boiling temperature which makes it perfect for us."

Garret looked at Holden. The pupils of his eyes were still elongated. They gazed at each other in silence for a moment, not even sharing a thought. The sexual tension stretched between them, drawn so tight Garret could barely breathe. It snapped with a flurry of movement as their bodies came together with an audible slap of hard muscled flesh grinding against each other. Garret kissed Holden with every ounce of expertise he had while letting go of the leash he'd had on his emotions and thoughts.

Hands cupped around the back of Holden's head, fingers in the short, soft inky strands of his mate's hair, Garret felt as if he was free-falling. The rush of adrenaline and loss of control that occurred when falling through the sky wasn't any different from how Holden's touch made him feel. His body pushed roughly against Holden's as their tongues danced together with heated urgency. Mindless with lust, Garret ground his hips against Holden's, the stiff thrust of his mate's cock rubbed against his with euphoric abandonment.

Somehow, and Garret was never quite sure afterward how exactly it happened because he could swear they never broke that kiss, they ended up on the flagstones beside the hot spring. Garret had Holden beneath him, kissing him deeply as their cocks pressed together with exquisite friction. Holden held him tightly, one hand gripping Garret's ass cheek while the other stroked his dragon clan mark. Their moans and pants grew louder than the bubble and splash of the hot spring as their pre-cum kicked up the friction of their cocks to a volcanic level.

Holden nipped Garret's tongue, causing Garret to finally break the kiss. He stared down at his mate seeing the smoke trailing from his nostrils and the passion that darkened his eyes.

"What?" he rasped, feeling Holden's fingers tracing the lines of his clan mark. He shivered as lust streaked through him, going straight to the throbbing cock he had pressed against Holden's.

With a flashing grin, Holden rolled Garret to his back, rising above him, their cocks still grinding together. "I never knew that grindage could be so fucking good," he murmured on a soft laugh. "Last night and now today."

"It's partly the connection," Garret panted as he peppered Holden's shoulders with hot open mouthed kisses and caresses. "Everything feels better when you can feel what your lover feels."

Shifting over onto his hip, Holden reached down and wrapped his fist around Garret's cock. Bolts of lust threaded through Garret and he groaned. The sounds of his pleasure seemed to please Holden because his amber eyes began to glow. Garret's heart thundered as he watched Holden. His mate stared fixedly at his hand stroking Garret's cock. He seemed almost mesmerized by the movement. Either that or he was studying the cock itself. Garret wasn't sure which and certainly wasn't in any mental condition to ponder the possibilities.

Holden bent and tentatively licked the tip of Garret's cock. The touch of his lover's inexpert tongue on his heated flesh sent a huge wave of emotion through every cell in Garret's body. He went completely still, waiting to see what Holden would do next. One hand reached down and cupped Garret's balls. They drew up tight in Holden's light grasp as Garret's arousal spiraled higher. Spreading his thighs wider and leaning back on his elbows, Garret gave Holden complete access to his cock, balls, and ass.

The tableau before Garret was like a painting. Filling the foreground was Holden's muscular, golden toned body, his classic profile topped by inky hair with an unruly shock that fell over his brow. The background of lush green trees dappled with sunlight made the whole scene seem almost surreal. Their stillness in this moment of discovery as Holden took his first steps toward true sexual reciprocity burned a snapshot of the interlude in Garret's mind forever. For the rest of his days, he would remember this moment and the awe that crept into his heart as the black dragon tried to show how he felt.

Holden glanced up and their eyes met. Garret could see the overwhelming lust that fired Holden's gaze, and he could also see the uncertainty lurking there. He reached out a hand and brushed the unruly spill of black hair back from Holden's brow.

"It's okay. Take your time. I want you to do only what you're ready to do," he murmured. "My body loves your touch. My heart craves it. But I never want you to regret a single moment with me."

Garret saw Holden's jaw clench at his words. His tongue came out and licked his lips, but his gaze didn't falter, holding Garret's steadily. "I'm not sure what I'm doing. This is all completely instinctual. I-I want to be with you. I crave it as much as you do," he said, his voice low and unsteady.

Holden's handsome face crinkled briefly in a self-mocking expression. "I want to do this, Garret, but you're going to have to help me a little. All I know about sucking cock is what I like. I don't know the logistics of it." A rough chuckle escaped him. "And afterward, I'm probably going to be on fire to fuck you."

A sense of inevitability fell over Garret. Holden wanted him. Everything would be okay. "Did you bring lube? I didn't think about it."

Holden laughed again, the sound still self-deprecating. "Yeah, I did. It seems my mind can't get over how good it was to fuck you last night. It keeps telling my cock to do it again."

Garret sucked in a breath. Fire licked at him from the writhing of his dragon inside. "Then do it. I loved the feeling of your cock inside me."

The dark head of his lover shook in a negative. "Not yet. I have to do this. I need to." Holden drew a shuddering breath. "By the gods, I *want* to, Garret."

With that, Holden bent and ran his tongue the length of Garret's cock. Pure bliss filled Garret's veins. He stroked his hand along the bulge of Holden's bicep as his lover used the flat of his tongue to tease Garret's cock. Holden's tongue explored every inch of Garret's hard flesh from the slit that oozed pre-cum to his achingly tight balls. By the time Holden lifted his head again, Garret shook from trying to stay still, trying not to frighten his new lover with the depths of his lust.

"Don't hold back, Garret. I'm not afraid of *you*. I'm afraid of what I feel and of not doing this right, not pleasing you," Holden growled with a little shake of his head. "I'm doing what I like to have done to me. Otherwise, I have no clue what the fuck I'm doing. I just know that I want this."

With that, Holden's head dropped and the heat of his mouth enveloped the thick head of Garret's cock. A loud moan escaped Garret and his eyes closed briefly on a wave of intense pleasure. Then he realized his mate struggled with something new and alien to him. Not just his emotional feelings for Garret but his sexual ones as well. Holden didn't know how to suck a cock, yet there he was, slurping away at Garret's.

A sense of unadulterated admiration came over Garret. He opened his eyes as Holden's mouth slid further down, taking more of the thick erection. Letting his heart and mind open fully to his mate, Garret brushed his fingers over Holden's hair, encouraging him...loving him.

"Easy, love. Don't rush it," he whispered. "Get used to the taste and the texture. Think about how much pleasure you're giving me. Can you feel it? You're my mate, my lover, the person I'm meant to spend my life with. Your touch inflames me and brings me more pleasure than I've ever known."

Holden paused, his golden eyes blinking unfocused at Garret for a moment. Garret didn't think he'd ever seen anything quite as erotic as the beautifully sculpted and incredibly handsome face and form of Holden Antaeus as he tasted cock for the first time. Held in the grip of lust, his mouth wrapped around Garret's thick erection, his thoughts bleeding out in a rush of pleasure, confusion, and unbearable passion, Holden was everything Garret had ever dreamed of in a lover. And he let Holden know that by not holding back a single thought or feeling.

The feverish glitter in Holden's eyes told Garret everything he needed to know. His lover wanted him fiercely, from his emotions and thoughts, to the stiff flesh Holden's mouth now caressed.

Tell me what you like, Garret. Help me suck your cock.

Holden's thoughts nearly made Garret come. He'd never known what someone was thinking or feeling while sucking his cock, but now he did in spades. The wonder and lust in Holden's head nearly sent Garret into a pleasure-induced coma. Knowing how much Holden liked sucking him, regardless of the differences between them, totally turned Garret on. It wasn't the most expert of blow jobs nor was it without the hesitancy one would expect of a newbie to the art. Holden sucked him with an innocent earthiness that fired Garret's passion for the man.

He gagged a few times and Garret had to explain how to relax his throat muscles, but Holden understood and put into practice all the advice. In fact he did so well, twisting his tongue around the length of Garret's cock while sucking, that Garret could hardly believe he'd never had a dick in his mouth before. There were some awkward moments and a slight scraping of teeth at one point, but Holden learned quickly and seemed to enjoy the act.

Some minutes after he'd first taken Garret's cock in his mouth, Holden looked up. Garret saw the intense heat in his mate's gaze and felt how aroused Holden had become from sucking his cock. He shivered as Holden's long fingered hands slid along his thighs caressingly. In that moment, staring into Holden's lust filled face, his cock sliding easily into his mate's mouth; Garret knew he was going to come.

He sucked in a harsh breath, his body tensing. "Holden. I'm going to come," he warned in a low breathless voice. "If you don't want your mouth filled, you'd best remove it from my dick *now*."

Holden winked at him and Garret felt the tip of his mate's tongue flick over the crown of his cock. Garret lost control. He sank his fingers tightly into Holden's silky black hair and thrust wildly into his lover's eager, untutored mouth. His cock swelled and then exploded, releasing a torrent of hot seed into Holden's mouth and throat. To give the man his due, he tried to swallow it all. A trickle escaped the corner of his mouth.

Garret collapsed on the flagstones, chest heaving, watching as Holden licked his now deflating cock. He couldn't remember ever having a blow job that made him feel so weak, and yet, so triumphant. He could tell from Holden's thoughts that his mate was pleased with himself. And truth be told, Garret was pretty proud of Holden too. He'd overcome a lot to get to the point of reciprocity so quickly.

Holden's hot body covered Garret's urgently. Wrapping his arms around his mate, Garret kissed him hard, their tongues twisting in a passionate dance of lust. He couldn't believe how turned on he was, even though he'd just had a huge orgasm.

Tearing his mouth away, Holden panted, "I need to fuck you, Garret. Sucking your cock just made me want you more. Seeing your dragon form, feeling you touch my cock while we were shifted turned me inside out. I want to fuck you so badly."

"Then do it," Garret told him with a smile. "I want whatever you want, Holden."

With a growl, Holden got up and dug in his backpack. As Garret sat up, Holden returned with the lube and their towels. He grinned at Garret and gestured toward the hot spring. "I think we'll try this with a little more than just lube."

Garret rose to his feet. "What did you have in mind?"

Holden dropped the towels and lube at the edge of the hot springs and stepped down into the steaming water. Cocking a brow up at Garret, he sat on one of the benches and spread his arms out along the rim of the pool. "I'm just gonna sit here. You're gonna sit on me, facing me."

The picture flashing through Garret's mind was hotter than the naturally heated spring. He stepped onto the ledge that Holden sat on. "If you want to do this, you're gonna need to get the lube out now, before I sink down into the water onto that cock of yours," he told his mate.

Holden reached for the lube and Garret bent at the waist, exposing himself to his lover. He heard Holden suck in a harsh breath. "Fuck. I don't know how long I can wait," he muttered.

Hiding a pleased grin, Garret said, "Then hurry. I can't wait to feel you inside me."

The cool slippery feel of the lube on his ass told him Holden didn't want to wait either. First one of his mate's fingers, then a second eased into his ass, spreading the lube carefully. The feel of Holden's fingers stroking him had his cock at half mast in moments despite having just come.

Garret pulled away from Holden's hand and straddled his thighs. Bracing his hands on Holden's shoulders, he slid down, his torso rubbing against his lover's. Desire lit flames in the black dragon's eyes as Garret slowed his descent, letting the head of Holden's cock brush his anus.

"You steer," he breathed roughly, leaning into Holden's chest as gravity pressed his ass against the thick cock of his mate.

One of Holden's hands grasped Garret's hip, the other slipped between their bodies, guiding his cock. Garret tilted his hips against Holden and drew a deep breath as the thick head of his lover's erection pressed past the tight ring of muscles into the hot, wet heat of his ass. He slid down inch by slow torturous burning inch until Holden's cock was firmly seated. Chests pressed together, they stared at each other wide eyed.

"You're amazing," Holden muttered.

"You're so fucking deep inside me, so close to me, I can feel your heartbeat," Garret said in soft amazement as Holden's hands slid up his wet back. He shivered.

Licking the side of Garret's neck, Holden murmured, "Shut up and let me fuck you already."

With a sly smile, Garret kissed Holden, his tongue stroking boldly, his mouth devouring as Holden's cock pressed deep within him. Their rhythm began slowly. Holden's hips rising, with Garret pressing into his mate's chest. Their kisses grew hotter. Their hands roamed every inch within reach whether wet or dry. The natural effervescence of the water lent itself to their slow, deliberate movements. Steam wrapped around them, mixing with the smoke that poured from their nostrils as their thrusts became harder.

Garret's dragon clawed at him from the inside. His dragon wanted out, wanted control, wanted to release his fire on Holden and sink his fangs into the thick muscle of his shoulder. He wanted his mate, wanted to belong to him completely.

Thrusting against Holden, feeling the thickness of his lover's cock spearing his ass and pressing against the exquisite bundle of nerves known as his prostate, blood filled Garret's groin and his own cock rose once more. As his mate fucked him, his swollen member rubbed against Holden's hard abs. The friction with the silky feel of the water all around made Garret moan in pleasure.

Holden nipped the underside of Garret's jaw. "Dear gods. Your ass is so tight and hot. I could fuck you like this forever," he growled, his golden eyes dazed with lust.

"You can," Garret replied breathlessly. "I'm your mate. You can fuck me whenever you like."

Holden's thrusts grew stronger and the water splashed more violently around them. Pleasure rocketed through Garret's body with every thrust. His every sense was tuned to the feel of Holden's cock in his ass. They kissed with fierce abandon, their bodies heating as only dragons could, adding to the steam in the air with great billowing puffs of smoke.

Drenched in sweat and mineral water, Garret's muscles strained as he rode Holden's thick cock. His lover growled, clutching the firm muscles of Garret's buttocks. Beneath Garret's hands, Holden trembled, his body shaking. Garret knew his mate was about to come. From the way he shook and moaned, Garret figured Holden would completely lose it.

He wasn't wrong.

Fingers digging deep into the flesh of Garret's ass, Holden thrust upward mightily, his head slamming back against the flagstones. His body shook like a tree in a hurricane force wind.

"Garret!" he yelled as he went rigid.

Riding the thick, spasming cock inside him, Garret felt the heated splash of his lover's cum fill his hot passage. One last press against his prostate, one more wet, twisting glide of his erection against Holden's ridged abs, had Garret crying out as his orgasm hit.

"Holden! Oh, gods!"

Shaking convulsively, his mind a dazed blank, Garret collapsed on Holden's chest. He nuzzled his lover tenderly, wanting to bite him too, taste his blood, bathe him in his fire, and mate him. The need to mate Holden was relentless. It fired his blood at the smallest whiff of Holden's lime scent or the mere thought of his taste or touch.

The hot spring bubbled around them, the hot water soothing against their over-stimulated skin. The point of Garret's chin rested on Holden's shoulder. He closed his eyes, savoring their closeness in the aftermath of their lovemaking. And for Garret it wasn't fucking. It was lovemaking. Emotions swelled within him and they revolved completely around Holden. What they had done had been anything but just sex.

"I could stay up here all day," he murmured groggily.

A chuckle rose from Holden, making his chest vibrate. "Just like this? With my cock in your ass?'

"Why not?" Garret sighed, feeling completely content. "You brought a whole tube of lube."

"Baby, your ass is bound to get sore after a bit. I've been fucking you hard."

Garret raised his head and his eyes met Holden's. "I'm not fragile. I won't break. I'm as strong as you are if not stronger."

Holden shifted uncomfortably. "This is not a repeat of last night, Garret. It was just a comment, mostly a joke. I'll fuck you just as much as you want me to."

"Really." The word wasn't even a question. It was more like a gauntlet tossed down between knights.

Black brows rose in a speculative expression. "Oh, yes. Really."

They stared at each other for long moments and Garret felt the emotion that coiled within Holden. Not everything was cut and dried for him the way it was for Garret. The conflicting emotions Holden bled out made Garret long to soothe his mate, but he knew Holden had to figure it out on his own.

With a sigh, Garret raised himself off Holden's body and floated on his back in the hot spring, feeling the soothing heat of the water seep into his pores. A splash indicated that Holden had left the bench. A hand brushed his thigh. He turned his head and met the golden eyes of his mate.

"I like being with you like this. The non-sexual, non-emotional moments," Holden said in a low voice. "I never had a best friend before. I like how this feels."

Astonishment whipped through Garret. "You've never had a best friend?"

Holden's shoulders moved in the water in what could have been a shrug. "No. Just my brothers and Eden." His eyes sharpened then. "Do you? Have a best friend?"

Garret sighed. Confession time. "No. I did have one once as a kid. However, he used me and it was all over after that."

"Used you?" Holden's eyes turned assessing.

Garret knew that the deepest secrets of his soul would be safe in Holden's keeping. The man was the epitome of integrity, but it was still difficult to tell those secrets. "I'm rather a brainiac, if you hadn't figured that out. All my life people have wanted to use me, exploit my intelligence to benefit themselves," he confessed. "Early on, I learned to surround myself with lots of friends. Good people, nice people. But they were people I never got particularly close to. They may have thought they were, but I always kept them at an emotional distance. My life is better if I never give people an opportunity to use me."

Holden's brows knitted in a fierce frown. "I'm so sorry, Garret. I would never use you." A wry smile tilted his mouth. "Your ass maybe, but I'd never use you for that whiz kid brain."

A laugh burst from Garret and he shocked himself at how carefree it was. "It will be nice to have a best friend, Holden."

His mate nodded. "I know. I like it a lot already. I never realized how much I envied Sean having two best friends. He, Declan, and Eden were always enough for me and I never understood why he was so close to Alfred and Marius."

"Alfred Stone and Marius Granville?" Garret asked a little surprised. A man like Sean Antaeus seemed like the last guy who'd have a best friend.

"Yeah. They've been best buds for years. They play golf twice a week." Holden replied. "Every industry event, the three of them have their heads together in a corner somewhere."

Garret filed the information away in his head to process later. He smiled at Holden then. "Why don't we head back since you're not a nature boy?"

"I wondered when you'd bring that up." A laugh escaped Holden as he maneuvered over to the bench. He climbed up and out of the water, steam rising from his wet, naked body. He reached for a towel as Garret climbed out of the pool.

They dried off and dressed, then headed back down the trail. Since they had to walk single file more than half the way down, they were silent, sharing a thought now and again. A warmth he'd never felt before spread through Garret's body. He could hear and sense Holden close on his heels. That nearness, the companionship they shared, how it had felt being goofy in their dragon forms in the glade, it all added up to a total sense of fulfillment within him. A self-satisfied smile spread across Garret's face as it dawned on him that he had never been so comfortable with another person on the planet, not even his parents.

Chapter Eight

For all that his comfort level with Garret had become fairly high, a core of confusion reigned inside Holden, and he kept it carefully locked away from his mate. He had questions for which he didn't think he could find answers. He definitely had the sense he was feeling his way around in the dark. Yet, at the same time, he felt confident that Garret was his mate, and his growing feelings for the green dragon were completely real.

But sexuality and having sex were two different things. Loving someone and being in love were two different things. Need, compulsion, belonging, compatibility, comfort, lust, all swirled within him, and he just couldn't get a handle on what exactly had happened to Holden Antaeus, the man. His dragon knew what he wanted and didn't really give a shit about the questions plaguing his logical brain.

When they got back to the lodge, by some silent, tacit agreement, they each went to their rooms to shower. Garret's mind and thoughts were completely open to Holden. He knew his mate was happy about what had happened at the hot springs. Holden kept his most private thoughts about the day to himself. He didn't want Garret getting the wrong idea while he sorted out how he really felt, but worry nagged him and he had no perspective whatsoever on what had occurred.

Dressed in fresh jeans and t-shirt, he emerged from his bedroom to find Garret on the hotel phone. He wanted to rub up against his lover's back, pressing his hips into Garret's firm buttocks, but he held off. Dressed in khaki shorts and a forest green polo shirt, the conservative green dragon was trying to soothe his boss, so Holden didn't think he'd appreciate being nuzzled and mussed up at the moment. Holden had already decided that Garret was a bit of a clothes whore, which was okay with him. Holden would love ripping at the man's clothes and ruffling Garret's composure as he ruined suits, silk ties, and expensive slacks in a sexual frenzy.

"Emily, I'm telling you this is nothing to panic over. The market will level off." Garret's voice held a sharp note and Holden knew his mate was biting the inside of his cheek to control himself. Frustration came off him in waves. "Just a minute." He covered the phone and whispered to Holden, "I'm probably going to her suite. She's in a snit over something Vahid said to her about an investment she made. Why does he have to pick on her so much?"

Holden shrugged. Vahid and Emily had always hated each other. Until recently, it had been a cold armed truce. Now, at the lodge, they were sniping at each other in a very uncontrolled way. Holden didn't know what had happened to set them off and until it interfered with business, he wasn't about to get involved.

"I'm going to see Declan. I'll catch up with you later," he said.

Garret nodded and returned to his conversation with Emily. Holden slipped out the door but instead of heading to his brothers' suite, he went down to the lobby and out to the hotel grounds. Pulling a cigar from his pocket, he lit it and began to prowl the wild beauty of the lodge gardens. As he walked, anger rose within him as the questions he'd locked within himself sprang free.

First and foremost was the fact that he'd just given in to lust. Lust driven by the need to mate. That clawing need inside him seemed to drive everything he'd done and felt over the past couple of days. The sense of being out of control filled him with fury and he wasn't sure why. Aside from the lust and being out of control, he didn't understand who he was anymore. His life had been so simple before. Now, the complications blurred his sense of self which frustrated him and fed right into the fury.

Holden stomped his way around the grounds of the lodge, puffing angrily on the cigar and wishing he had a flask of whiskey. What he needed was a stiff drink or five. Hell, he just needed to get totally shitfaced to even deal with what had happened. He couldn't believe what he'd done. What he'd done and liked.

Stopping beside a tree, he leaned against the trunk and took a long drag off the cigar. If he was honest with himself, he'd just flat out say that he'd loved sucking Garret's cock. The taste and texture had been new and exciting to him. Learning to take Garret's length and girth in his mouth had been a real eye opener too. He'd never realized what a talent cock sucking was. He didn't think he'd ever take a blow job for granted again. His free hand came up to rub his jaw, where the after affects of what he'd done still lingered with a slight soreness in the joint.

The cigar had removed the taste of Garret's cum from his mouth, but it hadn't removed his memory of it. Or of how it had felt when that thick shaft of flesh had trembled and jerked against his tongue, spewing the salty sweet essence of Garret into the depths of his mouth. It did nothing to remove his pleasure in Garret's orgasm and how much satisfaction he'd gotten from it.

Holden closed his eyes for a moment. Dear gods. This was all so much harder than he'd thought it would be. He'd started to get in the groove, started to accept what had happened, and then the first time he reciprocated, internally he flipped out, wondering once more just who he really was. Although he'd remained outwardly calm, Garret had to know that Holden blocked some thoughts from him.

Further along the path, Holden found a trash can and put the cigar out against the metal side, making sure nothing was smoldering before he tossed the stump in. A few feet away a gardener whacked at the bushes and brush, clearing it away. Holden watched in silence until a voice behind him said, "It's fire season."

Turning, he found an older Asian man standing on the path wearing the gardener uniform of the Gargoyle Lodge. He frowned a little. "I beg your pardon?"

The man smiled serenely. "You were watching my worker clear away the brush. He is doing so because it is fire season. We do the best we can to protect ourselves from wildfires by creating a distance between the grounds of the lodge and the rest of the forest."

"I see," Holden said thoughtfully, his eyes shifting from the Asian man to the man clearing the brush. "I hadn't realized."

The Asian man smiled enigmatically. "I know you didn't. But it's okay. You do now so you'll better understand going forward."

Holden turned back to the man clearing the brush. Somehow, he didn't think the man was talking about the brush anymore. "Going forward..." He repeated the words thoughtfully, his brain making the leap from what the gardener had said to his situation with Garret. Despite trying to accept Garret and learning to have sex with a man, he had been clearing away the brush in his mind to create some distance between himself and Garret. That distance would protect him from the emotional wildfire that threatened his peace of mind and sense of self.

Glancing over his shoulder at the Asian gardener, he realized the man had disappeared. Heading back down the path to the main lodge building, Holden knew he needed to get his head straight. For the moment, that meant he needed a little space, some time away from Garret. Taking the elevator, he went up to his brothers' suite. When he knocked on the door, Sean answered. Holden tensed.

"You and Declan need to get on those fucktards in Australia," Sean growled in his typical CEO voice. "They are holding everything up and it's costing me money. Did you see the projections the whiz kid gave me? That stock of theirs is taking a nose dive!"

Holden stepped into the suite and looked his brother in the eyes. "Sean, we always knew their stock prices would go down as soon as word of our takeover got out," he soothed. "And his name is Garret. Not whiz kid."

"Yeah, what-the-fuck ever," Sean muttered. "I just need this deal closed."

Fire began to burn in Holden's gut. As Sean moved toward the door, Holden stepped in his path, his furious amber gaze meeting his brother's. "No, not what-the-fuck-ever," he gritted out icily. "His name is Garret.

You will treat him with respect instead of the arrogance you usually dish out. He's not like anyone else you've ever hired so you better get that through your head now and treat him accordingly because if you don't, my fist and your nose have an appointment."

Sean's eyebrows shot up. "Is there something you want to tell me?" he asked harshly.

Holden nodded stiffly. "There is, but now is not the time."

Sean returned his nod. "Okay, then. When you're ready, I'll listen."

The door closed behind him and Holden drew a shaky breath. He walked over to the wet bar and poured himself a whiskey.

"What's wrong?"

The sound of his older brother's concerned voice brought an emotional lump to Holden's throat, just like when they'd been kids and he'd gotten hurt. Declan had always been the one to soothe him. If someone picked on him, Sean beat their asses and Declan took care of his tears, cuts, and bruises. Holden respected and loved Sean but the big brother he looked up to had always been Declan.

His older brother stood in the doorway to his bedroom, dressed in black sweats, bare-chested, with a towel slung around his neck. His black hair glistened with water and his clan mark swirled darkly over his shoulder and upper arm. Holden sighed and took his drink over to the sofa, plopping down wearily in the corner. Declan followed him, lowering his tall frame into the chair opposite Holden. He leaned forward, elbows on knees.

"Something's wrong. You might as well spit it out, Holden. I'm gonna get it out of you one way or the other," Declan said in a cool, logical voice. He gestured toward the glass of whiskey. "I can just keep plying you with those until you spill the beans."

"Fuck." Holden ran a hand around the back of his neck. Beans. Bean counter. Everything led back to Garret these days. He didn't know what to do or think any more. "I need some perspective, Declan."

His brother nodded and sat back. "I'm here. Tell me what's wrong."

Their eyes met and Holden remembered all the times Declan had helped him make up his mind from the type of bicycle he'd wanted as a kid to whether or not to go to Harvard Law School. He opened his mouth and said, "I found my mate."

Declan went very still. "Here? At the lodge? You met someone here?" He blinked, his dark brows slamming together. "But how? You've been spending all your time with the Won...der...boy..."

His voice trailed away as enlightenment dawned on his face. Holden nodded and the whole story poured forth, from the first moment he'd scented Garret to the moment he'd left him in the suite to go have a cigar. To give Declan his due, he didn't flinch or look surprised, although he had to be as shocked as Holden himself was.

When Holden's narrative ended and silence fell between them, Declan leaned forward again. His eyes raked over Holden searchingly. Unflinching beneath the knowing stare of his brother, Holden returned his gaze, letting Declan see the turmoil within him. A long sigh escaped Declan.

"You know, I always thought I would be the only one of us tortured in the mating game," he muttered. "I never figured that someone as happy and balanced as you would have any problems."

Declan's words told Holden that his brother had been unnerved by his tale. He never brought up his deathless infatuation with Elysia Granville. For him to refer to it now meant that what had happened to Holden had profoundly affected his brother.

Holden swallowed hard, but the lump in his throat wouldn't dislodge. "I'm confused, Declan," he said hoarsely. "I want him so much and being with him is so damned easy. He's like the best friend I never had."

His older brother nodded solemnly. "He fits you."

"Gods help me, but he does," Holden groaned, closing his eyes and letting his head flop back against the couch. When he opened his eyes, he found his brother gazing at him thoughtfully. "What?"

Declan smiled, the corner of his mouth lifting just a little. "Are you still attracted to women?"

Holden blinked in shock. He'd been so consumed with Garret that he hadn't even thought about that, but in actuality, it was at the root of his fears about his loss of self. Always before he'd known that he was attracted to women, that he was heterosexual. Now, because of the whole mating thing, he didn't know what the fuck he was or who he was any longer. "I-I don't know."

One of Declan's brows shot up. "If I put on porn, will you get aroused?" he asked curiously.

Glaring, Holden sat up on the couch. "No, because it's not exciting to watch porn with my brother," he replied in an acid tone. "Besides, I don't even wanna know why you have porn here."

Declan got up and went into his bedroom coming back with a DVD case. He tossed it at Holden who caught it automatically. "Take it back to your suite and play it. See if it winds you up." He shrugged. "You can assuage your horniness however you like, but it's a reasonable test."

Holden stared at the DVD. *Horny College Girls IV*. Great. His brother was giving him porn to determine if he was still interested in the opposite sex. What kind of help was that? "How is looking at porn going to help me? When you meet your mate your desire for anyone else wanes."

The smile on Declan's lips grew smirky. "Wanes being the operative word, Holden. You've only known about your mate a couple of days. You were prepared to fuck that gold digger this weekend before you met Garret. Wouldn't you like to know if you're still attracted to women?"

The confusion in Holden's brain grew worse with each of this brother's words. Garret had told him that mating had nothing to do with gender or sexuality. If that held true, then just because his mate was male didn't mean he was now gay. He should still be heterosexual, still find women attractive. The only man he should find attractive would be Garret. Although, he'd heard the debates on the "gay for you" issue, and while it might be applicable to humans, for dragons, mating bonds eliminated such debates.

"I don't understand all this stuff, Declan. It makes no sense to me," he muttered in a troubled voice. "Yeah, I'm beyond attracted to Garret. I feel the mating bonds pulling at me and I feel my emotions growing. My attachment to him is growing too. And the sex..."

Holden broke off as he caught a glimpse of his brother's face. He looked away with a sigh, saying gruffly, "I'm sorry. I wasn't really gonna go all TMI on you. Look, I know I'm not attracted to men. When I walk through the lobby or the bar, it's the women who draw my eyes, when I can manage to look away from Garret. I don't need your porn to tell me that."

Declan grinned. "Take it anyway. Maybe you'll find out some things about Garret by watching it with him." A thoughtful expression crossed his face and Holden wondered just what was going on inside his brother's head. "You know, it's pretty obvious that what you're feeling is specific to Garret. When I look at you, I don't see that you've changed at all. So your mate is a man? At least he's smart and talented and you get along with him. You have very compatible personalities. You'll probably be deliriously happy once you get over all the bullshit our society has fed you about sexual mores."

"What the hell, Declan? Why do you and Garret seem to think I've got my head up my ass about gender and being with a man?" Holden burst out angrily. Just because he needed some time to get his head straight about what had happened didn't mean he was against gay people.

His brother must have somehow known exactly what he was thinking. However, Holden knew he shouldn't be surprised, since Declan had always been that way with him. "Holden, I don't think this is about being gay or straight. This is about your mate. Taking the mate that is meant for you isn't about sexual roles or gender. It's about finding the one person on this planet who completes you in every way and makes you happier than anyone else ever could. It's not about sex."

Declan leaned forward, his eyes glittering as they met Holden's. "It's not about sex. It's about love, Holden," he said in a harsh whisper. "Do not fucking lose your chance here. You really don't want to be unhappy forever."

A strange, stark expression crossed Declan's face and Holden realized that his brother didn't expect to ever be happy. The face of his brother's torment calmed his fears. He would do whatever it took to make things work with Garret. He had to.

Rising to his feet, Holden held up the porn. "Thanks for the foreplay," he joked quietly.

Declan stood up, a lopsided grin on his face. "You're welcome. Enjoy it."

They walked to the door and Holden looked up at his older brother, noting the pain etched in eyes. "Some day, you will feel what I'm feeling," he said solemnly.

Declan shook his head. "The odds aren't good. But I want to see you happy. You're my little brother. The one I've always been responsible for." A little sigh escaped him. "I love you, Holden. Be happy."

Holden nodded, swallowing hard again as the lump in his throat returned. "I'm trying, Declan. I really am."

His brother patted his arm and opened the door, his expression turning businesslike. "I've got a conference call with Australia in a half hour. If I run into issues, I'll call you. I know you want to spend time with Garret, but this deal is hanging by a thread," he warned. "Don't be surprised if we end up working all night. It's why I tried to take a nap this afternoon. I have a bad feeling about this..."

Actually, Holden did too. He'd felt it all along. "Okay. I'll be ready, if you need me."

"Meaning I won't catch you in the middle of sex?" Declan said with a chuckle.

"No. Because if I'm in the middle of sex, I'm not answering the door or the phone," Holden replied easily, raising his brows in an amused expression.

"Got it."

Making his way back to his suite, Holden realized that his brother didn't see him any differently because he was now having sex with a man. That was a good thing and it gave him hope that he'd figure out his own confusion. He found the suite empty, a note from Garret tacked prominently to his bedroom door.

Gone to Emily's suite. Don't expect me back before dinner. Vahid really upset her.

There was no signature but obviously the note was from Garret. With a sigh, Holden went into his bedroom and shut the door. Maybe he needed a nap. Declan's warning about the Australia situation turning bad had him fretting a little about work and he hadn't had much sleep the night before. An hour's shut eye wouldn't hurt if tonight turned into a marathon of trying to save their takeover bid.

Stripping off his clothes, Holden turned on the TV for some background noise. His gaze fell on the DVD his brother had given him. On impulse, he popped it into the DVD player and stretched out on the sheets. For long moments he stared at the remote. Taking a deep breath, he turned on the porn.

Hot young women filled the screen. Naked women. Women kissing and sucking each other's tits. Women giving blow jobs. Ten minutes into the movie, Holden felt his cock stir. One woman, a redhead with a spill of russet curls, was sucking the cock of a really hung man while another woman licked her pussy and squeezed her breasts. The scene totally turned Holden on. He could just imagine his cock in her mouth instead of the porn actor's. And her tits were just spectacular, full and round, the pale pink nipples taut and straining.

With a groan, Holden found himself reaching for his cock. It was half hard and growing. Inside, his dragon growled and he stopped, his fingers mere inches from his hard flesh. Shit. He snapped off the DVD. The question of whether he still found women attractive was answered. But now that Garret was his mate, did he also find men attractive? The nagging sense that he needed to find himself pushed him to find the pay-per-view channels. He searched all the selections until he found a gay porn. Purchasing it, he waited impatiently for it to start.

Scenes of handsome hard bodied men came on the screen. Holden watched intently as they touched each other. A few minutes into the film, one muscle bound man began to suck the cock of another muscular man. Then they shifted to a sixty-nine. Minutes after that, one man was lubing the ass of the other. Holden stared at the screen as the men engaged in anal sex. With a sigh, he realized nothing had changed. He was still the Holden Antaeus he had always been. The men didn't arouse him at all.

He eyed the TV wondering if that was how he looked with Garret. As the porn actors fucked and sucked—two other men had entered the scene now—Holden thought about how he and Garret must look together. As he watched a blow job, noting that the man's cheeks hollowed with every suck, he wondered if he had looked like that while sucking Garret's cock. His groin filled with heat. The camera shifted to show the fucking couple and Holden's eyes were riveted by the shot of one man's cock moving in and out of the generously lubed ass of the other man. Gods! He and Garret had looked like that!

Holden's cock stirred as he imagined the fucking couple as himself and Garret. Now, his dragon howled with lust, wanting Garret as much as Holden did. This time he gripped his cock and thought about how he felt being with Garret. The men on the screen moaned and sucked and fucked, but Holden's head was filled with visions of himself touching Garret, of Garret touching him, of how excited he'd been to suck Garret's cock...

I need to shut you off. I can't work. All I want to do is race back to the suite and touch you.

Holden groaned out loud at Garret's thoughts suddenly entering his head. *I'm totally jacking off to thoughts of us being together.*

I know and it's driving me insane because I'm busy right now. But later, Holden, later I'll—

Holden cut him off. *Get back to work. Later, we'll probably have the Australian takeover to deal with. But after that, I've got something to show you.*

If it's what's in your hand right now, I can hardly wait.

Holden shut down the communication between them, letting Garret get back to work. He turned off the TV and closed his eyes, his hand stroking his stiff erection, the erection he had gotten from thinking about Garret. It was clear to him now. He was still the same man he had always been. He was attracted to women...and to Garret. Other men held no interest for him and women didn't much interest him anymore either. He finally acknowledged what was growing in his heart. He'd fallen in love with Garret Renquist.

Chapter Nine

Lips trailed down Holden's spine, caressing his clan mark. He stretched, his naked body arcing toward the lips that left a trail of fire along his skin. A pair of hard hands smoothed over his thighs and hips, squeezing his buttocks briefly.

"One day, when you've fully accepted what this is between us, I'll fuck you. And then you'll know what it means to be my mate, Holden. To share everything with me."

The sibilant whisper trailed warm air over Holden's spine and he shivered. Already, much of him belonged to Garret. The man's presence filled all the empty spots inside him and brightened all the dark places. Everything he'd ever thought about having a mate had been blown to pieces by Garret. The calm acceptance of what life had handed them showcased the keen intelligence of the man. His wicked sense of humor suited Holden's fun side. His conservative, stuffy British side served to make Holden want to crack his composure, to watch the cool exterior be replaced by a fire storm of lust.

Holden rolled over to find Garret sitting on the side of the bed. Their eyes met and then Garret's dropped to take in Holden's partially erect cock. With a resigned sigh, Garret said, "Your brother's here. There's trouble in Australia."

"Why didn't you wake me sooner? We could have..." Holden's uneven voice broke off as Garret shook his head.

"I'd only just gotten here when Declan knocked."

The regret in his eyes triggered a flood of emotion inside Holden. Sitting up, he reached out and wrapped a hand around the back of Garret's head, pulling him in for a hot kiss. As their lips parted, Holden groaned. "Damn it. I'll get dressed. Tell Declan I'll be right there."

Garret got up and went to the door, his eyes on Holden's body as he stretched once more. Then he was gone. Holden's clan mark still tingled from Garret's touch. If nothing else convinced him who his mate was, the response of his clan mark surely did. The instant Garret touched his mark, his dragon went nuts wanting to mate him.

In Holden's head, the vision of them in their dragon forms, cocks unsheathed in mating heat, filled his head. The afternoon in the glade had been so primal that Holden knew one day they probably would have sex in shifted form. Dragon sex was raw and rough, but between males it was a lot easier to accomplish because there was no fear of hurting your partner. With a female, who was much smaller, one snap of your tail could break her bones. Since Holden always liked his sex on the raw and rough side, being with a man certainly made things a lot easier.

When he stepped out of his bedroom, he found Declan and Garret deep in a discussion of the Australian company's finances. Holden grabbed a couple of bottles of water from the wet bar and sat down beside Garret, handing him one automatically. He looked up to find Declan's eyes watching him with a wry expression.

"So tell me what happened," he said coolly.

Declan launched into a litany of the problems that had surfaced in the past twelve hours with their takeover of the Australian funeral home company. An hour later, a knock on the door brought Sean and Emily into their strategy session. Declan kept making calls. Garret kept crunching numbers and Holden kept shaking his head over the other company's demands.

By three a.m., Sean poured himself a shot of whiskey and knocked it back. "Look. If they don't want to make this easy, I'll just take their choices from them," he growled angrily. "I don't appreciate their whining and the way they're trying to negotiate as if this were a merger. It's not a fucking merger. It's a takeover. If they push me anymore, it will be a hostile takeover." Sean's eyes speared Garret. "We are in a position to just take them, aren't we?"

Garret nodded. "You could indeed. It would save you quite a bit of time to go that route as well. Although it does strain relations when you walk in the door as the new owner."

Smoke rolled from Sean's nostrils. His hawk-like expression sharpened and his gaze settled on Declan. "Make it so. I'm tired of their shit. They could have had the easy fuck, but they've pissed me off now. Bend them over. The bastards."

He stormed from the suite with Emily on his heels and Declan stood up. "You heard the boss. Seducing didn't work. Time to rape and pillage," he joked tiredly. "I'll put the wheels in motion before I go to bed. I'll see you both at brunch. It's a good thing we start late tomorrow. I'm wiped. G'night!"

Silence fell when Declan left. Holden heaved a sigh and stretched out his legs, draping his arms along the back of the sofa. "Fuck if that wasn't just a waste of freaking time," he grumbled.

Garret stood up and took his wine glass over to the bar, pouring the last of the bottle into the glass. He stood leaning on the bar, sipping his drink. Holden watched him, noting that he still looked as crisp as he had earlier in the day. It made Holden long to muss him up.

"It's unfortunate that they are so stubborn. It's truly not to their advantage," Garret said quietly.

"You should never try to dictate to someone stronger than you," Holden agreed.

Garret finished his wine and set the glass down. "Now what?" he asked.

Holden's brows rose. "Bedtime for all brand new mates," he grunted as he rose to his feet. He started toward his bedroom but stopped when Garret didn't move. "Is something wrong?"

The smile that sent pleasure licking at Holden's veins flashed out. "No. But we've spent a couple of days fucking. It's late. I think sleep is in order."

Holden snorted and sauntered over to Garret, grasping his chin in one long fingered hand. He could feel the rasp of Garret's beard against his fingertips. "Did I say anything about fucking? I can tell that you're tired, Garret. Let's go to bed, okay?"

Tilting his head, Holden kissed Garret squarely on the mouth. Their tongues tangled slowly. Holden sucked on Garret's tongue then pulled away. "Bed. Let's go to bed."

Garret nodded and they went into Holden's bedroom. Stripping off their clothes, they tumbled into bed, Holden spooning Garret as they had the night before. Contentment seeped into the marrow of Holden's bones. He buried his face in Garret's short hair, breathing in the scent that belonged only to his mate. Every muscle in his body went limp as total relaxation came over him. Curled into Garret's back, he fell asleep.

~ * * * ~

Waking with his body pressed to hard planes, angles, and muscles still seemed a bit alien to Garret. He'd rarely spent the entire night with anyone, so the past couple of mornings had seemed strange to him. He'd not let on to Holden how odd it was, because every atom in his body was set to soothe his mate's fears and confusion.

Mostly, Garret accepted that he'd found his mate. He accepted those feelings inside himself that grew every time his nostrils caught a whiff of Holden's unique lime scent or his glance filled with Holden's lean muscles or mocking smile. The gnawing ache inside when his dragon demanded to mate Holden had been easy to accept, even if it made him feel desperate at times.

He'd fallen into such an easy camaraderie with his new mate, had been so comfortable with him, and so happy with the sense of contentment he now felt, that he'd not focused on other emotions. In that first frantic night of sex and discovery, he'd said the word that had risen to the top of his brain as soon as he'd known Holden wasn't going to push him away. It was true that he loved Holden. He had almost from the moment he'd met him. A man like Holden was easy to fall for. However, the ground swell of emotion inside him now, after more than two days in his new mate's company, was a far cry from that initial sense of love he'd had.

In his heart, Garret knew that this man was meant to be his, just as he was meant to be Holden's. The love he felt for Holden became larger and more firmly entrenched in his heart with every touch, every glance from those golden eyes. Garret had lost his soul to the black dragon and he didn't know what he would do if Holden didn't feel the same way.

Usually, Garret never let fear dictate to him. He let it advise him to use caution, but he never let fear gain the upper hand inside him. With Holden vacillating and trying to find answers to things that just were, Garret had allowed fear to gnaw at a small core of insecurities within him. He worried that things had moved too quickly for Holden. He worried about what would happen when they returned to the city and to their regular lives. He worried about fitting into Holden's life. And he worried about Holden never saying, "I love you."

The heat of Holden's body against his, lax in sleep, made Garret's emotions hard to ignore. Lying in the warmth of their bed, their naked bodies pressed together as if they couldn't bear not to touch, made Garret's heart pound with the force of his love for his mate. When Holden was awake, Garret had to corral and contain those feelings to keep from overwhelming the one person he couldn't afford to alienate. Now, while Holden slept, Garret could give those emotions free reign.

He nuzzled his face into the curve of Holden's hard shoulder as his hands softly stroked the hair roughened skin of his lover's thighs. His palms glided over the smooth hips and lean curves of Holden's glutes. The scent of limes permeated the air, filling Garret with so much love that he didn't think he could bear it if something happened to made this new relationship go sour.

Garret knew statistics, how to work the numbers. He calculated risk daily in his job. Calculating the risk of Holden never figuring out the whole gay-straight-mates thing scared Garret in part because it wasn't exactly quantifiable. For the first time in his life, he wanted something that he couldn't just plan to accomplish. Literally, from one moment to the next, he was unsure whether Holden would bolt, refusing to accept that his mate was a man, refusing to accept Garret's love, refusing to love Garret back.

And that was it in a nutshell for Garret. He could lay his heart and soul at Holden's feet, but would he ever receive Holden's in return? Would Holden ever love him?

His arms tightened convulsively around his lover as his chest tightened painfully, an ache forming behind his breast bone. *I just want you to love me back,* he thought fiercely. *You don't even have to love me as much as I love you. Just a little would be okay. It would be enough...*

But really, Garret knew it wouldn't be enough. He wanted all of Holden. And he knew there was a very good chance that it would never happen.

Holden stirred and Garret fought to get his emotions under control before Holden's brain awoke enough to hear and feel them. Heat fired Garret's veins as Holden's hips pressed into his, unconsciously humping him. His cock swelled as he felt Holden's slide against it.

"Mmmn. A hard man is good to find," Holden joked sleepily as he rotated his hips, his erection grinding deliberately against Garret's growing one.

"You're a quick study," Garret teased with a soft laugh.

Holden's eyes opened. The amber irises were dark, the pupils elongated. Amusement, contentment and an indefinable emotion swirled in their depths. Garret's heart thundered. Holden felt something for him. It was there in his eyes. Whether he could capitalize on that and make it grow...well, it was like tending stock...volatile, exciting, and filled with promise.

"One of the things I always hated about spending the night with someone is that in the morning, when I wanted to fuck, I'd have to race to the bathroom to brush my teeth," Holden complained.

"Are you trying to tell me you want to get up and brush your teeth so we can fuck?"

A laugh escaped Holden as his hands began to caress Garret's chest and shoulders. "Isn't it obvious?" His stiff penis pushed against Garret's boldly.

Pushing Holden onto his back, Garret sat up in the bed. "You're a dragon. You don't need to brush your teeth. You have built in mechanisms for ridding your mouth of germs and smelly bacteria," he said with a grin. "I'm surprised you didn't think of it."

Drawing a breath, smoke pouring from his nostrils, Garret opened his mouth and a lick of flame came out, but was immediately sucked back into his mouth. A black puff of smoke came out his nose as he swallowed hard, feeling the fire burn its way through his mouth and down his throat.

Holden gazed at him with an astonished, impressed expression on his face. "Did you just swallow a fireball?"

Garret nodded and grinned. He blew out a stream of air into Holden's face. It smelled slightly like burned toast, but definitely was not morning breath. Holden's brows rose as he sat up, the sheet falling to his hips.

"I gotta try this," he said with a grin.

Garret smiled, watching Holden swallow the fireball, black smoke coming from his nostrils in a burst. His mate's grin was wider than the Mississippi and he looked thoroughly pleased with himself. Holden blew out a breath that had only a hint of fire and brimstone to it and nothing of morning breath.

Holden laughed and sexual flames lit his eyes as he reached down to shove the sheet back. Garret sucked in a breath as his mate's hand closed around his cock, stroking it with a twisting motion.

"You're pretty bold for a man who'd never given a blow job until yesterday," Garret said, his breath hitching a little as Holden's hand fired his groin with heat-laden lust.

Holden shifted toward him, leaning in until their mouths were only inches apart. "Yeah, well, maybe you need to teach me something new today since I'm such a quick study. How about we take this into the bathroom? To the tub?"

Garret shook his head. "I don't think so. A lesson in *soixante neuf* is always best given on a firm mattress."

"Sixty-nine? Damn. A man after my own libido," Holden replied, a grin breaking out on his handsome face.

"That is more true than you know, Holden," Garret murmured and closed the distance between them.

Taking Holden's mouth in a hot kiss, Garret sucked his lover's tongue as his dragon again clawed at him, reminding him of the need to mate Holden. The taste of Holden's lips and tongue inflamed him. With a growl, Garret pressed Holden down onto the bed, covering his body and kissing him with fierce pleasure. Ignoring the rasp of their beard roughened cheeks and jaws they kissed with a passion that had grown exponentially since that first angry kiss. Now they knew each other's taste and texture, what made them moan and twist frantically with lust.

Holden held the back of Garret's head as if he couldn't bear for him to move away. The gesture made Garret's already thundering heart ache with love for his mate. Beneath him, Holden writhed, his lean hips arcing up so that their cocks rubbed in delicious friction. It took all of Garret's considerable self-control not to tear his mouth from Holden's and tell the man how much he loved him. Instead, he channeled that emotion into his kiss and prayed to the gods that Holden would eventually feel the same.

Feeling the wetness of their pre-cum lubricating each thrust of their hips, Garret broke the kiss. "If we keep this up, I won't last to show you how to do a sixty-nine," he groaned breathlessly.

"By all means, professor. Show me what I need to do," Holden replied, his breath coming just as quickly and unevenly as Garret's.

"As you know, the person on top has all the control," Garret began, trying to gather his scattered wits as Holden peppered his jaw, throat, neck and shoulders with hard, biting kisses. "Since you're new to this with a man, you'll need to be on top so that you're not forced to take more than you can handle."

With an impressive flex of muscle, Holden rolled them so that Garret was pressed into the mattress. Pinning Garret down with knees, hands and weight, Holden deliberately stroked his cock against Garret's, then pressed it against his ass. Garret shuddered with bliss. Another moment and he'd forget all about the sixty-nine lesson and beg Holden to fuck him. He loved the feel of his lover's cock in his ass, loved the feel of belonging to Holden.

"Since I'm on top, I can make you take all of me. If I'm pinning you down, you can't get away. You have to suck me. All of me," Holden stated, smoke coming from his nostrils.

Obviously, the thought of being in control heightened his arousal. Garret decided to play to that. "Yes. The person on top doesn't even have to suck the cock of the person beneath him. He can tease him, lick him, stroke him, and not actually ever get to the sucking."

Holden groaned loudly, his eyes filled with amber fire. "I want you," he breathed. "Suck me, Garret."

Knowing that the position wasn't the easiest thing to accomplish the first time, Garret pushed the pillows beneath his head and shoulders as Holden turned his body, his knees straddling Garret's head. His engorged penis brushed across Garret's face and a delirious groan escaped him, making Garret smile.

As Holden's body stretched above him, Garret tilted his head back slightly and guided the long, thick length of his mate's cock toward his mouth. His tongue flicked out, catching the latest surge of pre-cum drops from the slit in the head. Parting his lips as Holden pressed down toward his face, Garret felt the smooth hard flesh slide into his mouth. His hands slid up the back of Holden's thighs to tease his balls.

"Oh, fuck, Garret!" Holden's voice cracked on a moan.

Feeling inspired, Garret sucked avidly on Holden's cock as his fingers went to work teasing his lover's ass, rubbing and stroking his sensitive anus.

"Holy fuck! How am I supposed to suck you when you do that to me?" Now, Holden's voice trembled with lust and despite the dick in his mouth, Garret grinned in triumph.

He wound his tongue around Holden's stiff cock, teasing every inch of it as he sucked. Meanwhile, his fingers and thumbs stroked the sensitive area from Holden's balls to his anus. He was so into driving Holden crazy with desire that he'd forgotten it was supposed to be a sixty-nine. Just as Garret was about to press a finger into Holden's ass, his mate sucked the head of Garret's cock into his mouth.

The most delicious heat flooded the lower half of his body as Holden began to suck his cock. His fingers dug into the muscles of Holden's thighs as he tried to suck in concert with his lover. Long minutes passed, the sound of sucking and muffled moans soft in the morning stillness. Garret's balls drew tight to his body, the ache in them telling him that his orgasm wasn't far off. Holden's cock swelled in his mouth, a sure sign he wasn't far from coming either. Garret brushed his fingers over Holden's perineum, feeling how his mate's body shook and trembled. He probed Holden's anus carefully, teasing it over and over until he felt the ring of muscles relax. He slid the tip of a finger into Holden's ass and his lover jerked and stiffened. With a muffled cry that vibrated against Garret's cock, Holden came.

Garret thrust his finger further into Holden, causing him to shudder. Sucking and swallowing Holden's cum while his lover sucked and licked him and gently pulled his balls, sent Garret careening over the edge. Thrusting his hips up and pressing more of his cock into the wet suction of Holden's mouth, Garret came with a fierceness he had only ever experienced with his mate. He didn't think about whether Holden could handle it or whether it choked him. The only thought in his mind was how much he loved Holden.

The aftermath of the *soixante neuf* lesson was a soak in the huge Jacuzzi tub. Trying to fit two muscular men over six feet tall into the tub took a little maneuvering, but Garret was content to sit in the cradle of Holden's thighs, resting against his mate's body.

"You know, I think I've had more sex the past few days than I intended to have had I gone to that spa," Holden joked.

Garret barely kept himself from stiffening. He didn't want to think about Holden's life and how things would work when they returned to the city. He wished he could be more self-assured, but that core inside him, the place he had yet to let Holden see, was riddled with doubt.

"The sex is awesome. After we're done today, I think we should reward ourselves with more sex," he replied in a teasing tone.

"That reminds me. I've got something to show you tonight. I think it will be our foreplay."

Holden's laugh held a note of mocking amusement and Garret wondered what it was that he had to show. However, he lacked the confidence to just ask. Besides, if they didn't hurry, they'd be late for brunch. When he said that to Holden, a string of curses left his mate's mouth.

As they dried off, Garret asked, "Do you have a thing about being late or something?"

Holden sighed. "Yes. It irks me when others are late and I really hate it when I am. Besides, Sean's stare is lethal if you walk into one of his meetings late. He totally shreds you with a glance," he confessed.

"Then we better hurry." Garret pointed to his watch.

Holden's eyes widened and then he became a flurry of activity, rushing into his bedroom and grabbing briefs and socks. With a grin, Garret followed more slowly and reached out to stroke his palm over Holden's firm buttock as he passed by. Holden growled but he couldn't very well do anything about Garret's teasing caress while hopping on one foot to pull on his socks.

Laughing, Garret retreated to his room. A glance at the day's itinerary showed brunch with a scheduled seminar followed by another seminar that split them into two groups. Holden and Garret were not in the same group for the second seminar. Deciding to take a leaf from Holden's book, Garret dressed in jeans and a t-shirt, but instead of leaving his shirt loose like Holden he neatly tucked it in and smoothed it down inside his jeans. He knew Holden thought he was rather prissy about clothes, and perhaps he was, but he didn't consider it a bad habit.

With his organizer in hand, he went to meet Holden and they hurried down to the dining room together. Today it was set up with a podium for the speaker. They grabbed plates of food from the buffet and sat down just as the seminar began. Garret noticed immediately that both Sean and Declan were missing from the group. As he speared a strawberry, he wondered how the takeover was going.

Before his thoughts could get very far, Sean and Declan slipped into the room, taking the empty seats on the other side of Garret. Declan reached for the pot of coffee on the table in front of them and poured for himself and Sean. Holden looked around Garret at his brothers and his expression tightened. Sean's face had a hawk-like, enigmatic expression that heralded trouble. Declan just looked wiped out and pissed off.

Garret's stomach sank. He had a feeling the rest of the day would be spent trying to get the takeover of the Australian funeral home corporation accomplished.

Sure enough, as soon as the seminar was over, everyone left to go to the next one, but Emily, Sean, Declan, and Vahid stayed behind. A waiter set two plates of steaming food in front of Sean and Declan.

"Sit down," Sean said, waving a fork with a sausage on it at them. Once everyone was seated he sipped his coffee, looking at them. "I don't want to have to do this, but someone's got to go to Australia. We'll finish out the retreat, but as soon as it's done, we're headed home. Vahid, you need to make sure every part of this retreat continues to go off as it is supposed to. When it's over, I need you to ensure that not one of these problems leaks out."

Sean paused and took a few more bites of his breakfast. "Emily, you're going home to pack. Declan and Holden are too. I'm sending the three of you to Australia to fix this mess. I want that goddamned company. I no longer care what it takes to get them. You bully them. You fuck with them. You shove them up against the wall and rape them anally. I don't fucking care," he growled, smoke coming from his nostrils. "No one tries to pull the wool over the eyes of an Antaeus. They could have been taken over nicely. Now they've lost the right to an easy takeover. This is beyond hostile. This is flat out war. We will conquer them until they all run home to mommy wearing American made panties."

Garret's eyes widened. He'd seen pissed off CEO's before but Sean Antaeus went into a whole new realm of pissed off. As soon as Sean stopped talking, Declan began. He went over every detail, making sure that each of them knew what they needed to do, what information they needed to gather, and who would do what while the three executives were gone.

When Vahid began going into details of the flights that his assistant had booked, Garret realized that not only would he be walking into the office as the head of the finance department on Monday morning, since Emily would be out of the office on her way to Australia, but he would be without Holden too. A separation so soon in their relationship wasn't a good thing. Fear stabbed deep within him in the place where his doubt lived. Holden's trip would be the biggest test of their new relationship and Garret wasn't sure what the outcome would be.

Chapter Ten

Unhappy didn't describe how Holden felt. He wanted to shoot Sean. He'd just found Garret and now he had to go to fucking Australia. All because Declan and Sean had initially chosen to be nice to the Australian corporation they were taking over. They'd gone up to Declan and Sean's suite, leaving Emily and Garret with Vahid to work out the details of running the finance department in Emily's absence. Sean and Declan were arguing about the Australian company's executives. Holden just wanted to grab Garret and go home. Already his head pounded with frustration.

"What are you so pissed about?" Sean barked suddenly.

Coming out of his angry thoughts, Holden looked up at his older brother. Strangely, the expression in Sean's eyes seemed worried.

Holden frowned. "What would you know about me being pissed? And when did my emotions and feelings ever matter when it came to work?" he snapped.

Sean's eyes flared, but it wasn't with heat. Holden couldn't figure out exactly what his expression meant. "You're my brother and I care about you. If something is wrong, tell me so we can try to keep work from interfering too much," Sean replied quietly.

Holden turned his head and looked at Declan who shook his head infinitesimally. So Declan hadn't said anything to Sean about Garret. Holden's gaze returned to the head of the family. Sean seemed to know something was going on in Holden's life but if Declan hadn't spilled the beans, Holden had no clue how Sean could know anything.

"Why are you saying this to me, Sean?"

With a little growl, Sean sat down in a chair, his gaze settling on Holden. "You've been different since we've been here. Something's up. You said you had something to tell me but weren't ready yet. You're out of time now. Tell me what's going on and how Garret Renquist fits in the picture," he said coolly.

Startled, Holden blinked in surprise. "He's my mate." The words came out boldly. Holden had wanted to ease into the explanation when the time came to tell Sean, but somehow, the stark words just slipped out.

Expecting some kind of stupendous reaction from Sean, Holden watched as his older brother just nodded, his expression unchanged. "And you don't want to leave him yet. I understand," Sean replied quietly. "I remember feeling the same when Careen and I first got together." A wry expression settled on Sean's hawkish features. "Hell, I still hate being away from her."

"You hate being horny without an outlet." Declan's deep voice, tinged with wry amusement entered the conversation.

Holden looked up as Declan lowered his tall frame to the couch. Sean laughed, a short self-deprecating laugh. "It's true. I've been mated so long I think I've forgotten how to masturbate."

With a groan, Holden covered his eyes. "Oh, gods. First Declan and his porn and now you and the masturbation remark. Way too much TMI, brothers," he complained.

Sean and Declan laughed. "Damn. And I was going to ask you about the whole prostate erogenous zone thing," Sean joked.

As Holden uncovered his eyes about to snap out a retort, Declan muttered, "It's true. Just don't ask how I know."

Eyes widening, Holden stared at his older brother. "You and...?" He broke off, unable to even fathom the idea that Declan was bi-sexual.

Declan shook his head. "Not a man, Holden. And I think that's about all I'm willing to say on this subject. You're the one who howled TMI, remember?"

Sean heaved a sigh. "I'm sorry, Holden. There isn't much I can do. Declan needs you on this. However, when the two of you have things pinned down to the point that Brian can take over for you, by all means come home and take a few days off. Meanwhile, we'll keep an eye on your mate for you."

"Please don't take him to strip clubs," Holden groaned. "I know he'd probably love it, but just...don't."

Sean laughed. "I can't get Alfred to go to one. What makes you think I can get Wonderboy to? No one will go with me."

"No one wants to risk the wrath of Careen if they do," Holden said with a grimace.

The rest of the afternoon was spent preparing for the trip to Australia. By the time Holden made it back to his suite, he was exhausted. He found Garret stretched out on a lounger on the balcony in a pair of shorts and nothing else, a brown bottle of ale on the table at his side, soaking up the last rays of the late afternoon sun.

Holden stripped all his clothes off and tossed them on the couch before joining Garret on the balcony. He stretched out on the other lounger, feeling the sun's warmth seep into his naked skin.

"That lounger is not very sanitary, Holden."

"Don't care. Sun feels good," he muttered.

"Does that mean I get to sanitize your ass so you're not covered in dirt and germs from that thing?" Garret asked with a chuckle.

"Sure." Holden turned his head and looked at his lover. Garret's body was relaxed, but there was a hint of anxiety in his deep green eyes. "We have some things to settle before I leave for Australia."

The green eyes suddenly became hooded. "We do?"

"Yeah." Holden reached out and took Garret's beer, taking a sip before putting it back on the table between them. "You're staying in a hotel right? Until you can find somewhere to live?" Garret nodded cautiously and Holden smiled. "Not any more. As soon as we get back, we'll pick up your things and go to my place. You don't need to find a place. You're my mate. You'll live with me. My penthouse condo is everything you said you wanted in a place, ocean view, but close to the office. It's perfect."

Garret's expression stayed closed off. "Okay."

Holden cocked an eyebrow up at him. "I like the idea of knowing that while I'm gone your naked ass will be in my bed." He shot Garret another smile. "You can drive my car while I'm gone. Go car shopping. This is California, baby. You need wheels."

"Okay," Garret said again, this time with a little sigh.

Holden sat up, his gaze holding Garret's. "What's wrong?"

For a long moment, Garret didn't reply. Finally, three words burst from him, "I'll miss you."

Holden's heart felt as if it somersaulted in his chest. "I'll miss you too," he said softly. "Look, I'm done with this fucking retreat. How about we order up some dinner and watch a movie?"

Holden didn't want to tell Garret what kind of movie, he just thought he'd put the idea out there and explain later. When Garret flashed that brilliant smile, Holden's stomach dipped as it always did, but now, he welcomed the feeling in a way he hadn't the first couple of days. What had happened between them in the past twenty-four hours—both between him and Garret and his own discoveries—made all the difference to Holden.

They soaked up the sun until it grew dark then ordered room service. Holden pulled on his jeans as a concession to the room service waiters and began packing to go home. He knew that mentally, they were both exhausted. What had happened to them had been swift and overwhelming. Now, work and everyday life intruded on their discovery.

In Holden's mind, he had accepted Garret as his mate. However, he needed time before actually mating him. His logical brain wanted all the roadblocks removed before he bathed Garret in his fire and accepted his fire in return. They needed to settle into daily life and let their families and co-workers become accustomed to them as a couple. They needed to let their feelings ferment and grow so that speaking of love had no hesitancy or uncertainty about it.

The fact that Holden had to leave for an unknown number of days, threw a monkey wrench into his plans. He didn't like the fact that almost as soon as he and Garret got home, he would have to leave. All the things he'd thought about doing with Garret when they got home wouldn't happen now because of the mess in Australia, and Holden was beyond disappointed.

By the time dinner arrived, they were both packed and ready to leave in the morning. Holden knew that Garret had ridden up to Gargoyle Lodge with Emily so there were no obstacles to them leaving together. They got along so well that Holden actually looked forward to the drive, anticipating they'd spend the time getting to know each other better. He was eager for Garret to see his condo and wondered what he would think of it. Holden sucked at decorating so he knew there would be some work ahead of them to actually make the place look like someone with a personality lived there. He knew Garret was a bit of a clothes whore but didn't know if his sense of style extended to furniture.

Over dinner and a bottle of wine he discovered that Garret didn't have any talent for fixing up a bachelor pad either. They made a list of furniture they would need and what would need to go. Garret worked from home often and preferred to have a comfortable desk. They decided that since they both sucked at figuring out how to put a home together that they would ask Sean's wife Careen for help.

Holden could tell that Garret seemed nervous about Declan and Sean knowing the truth about them, but he wasn't worried. His brothers would love whoever he loved. It was really that simple.

"My family is nothing to be nervous about, you know. Mates are important to us. Our parents defied their families to be together so we're all acutely cognizant of how important mates are," Holden explained as they dug into the chocolate cake he'd ordered.

Garret's brows rose. "Your grandparents didn't want them to be together? Even though they were mates? How odd."

Holden nodded. "Our father came from a very old black clan. Apparently, his father was quite a stickler for clean bloodlines. The Antaeus name is very old. Our mother's family was even older, but old man Antaeus refused to accept her." He shrugged. "He had the color prejudice."

"Your mother wasn't a black dragon?" Garret looked surprised.

Shaking his head, Holden chuckled. "Have you ever seen a black dragon with eyes like ours?" he teased. "Our mother was a red. Her family disowned her for mating with an upstart black dragon."

"So the feud between your parents' families fueled your desire to study dragon anthropology?' Garret asked curiously. He licked icing off his fork and Holden's groin tightened watching the movement of his tongue. The things that man could do with his tongue drove Holden crazy with lust. Just watching him lick icing turned Holden's libido into a raging fiend, and his dragon into an insistent nag wanting only to mate Garret.

"Maybe a little. Our parents didn't believe in the whole color clan thing. They always maintained that the divisions had come about through culture and not nature. I agree. And regardless of the dire warnings of their parents, my parents were deliriously happy together. In fact, Emily is distantly related to us somehow on our mother's side. When she left her family, Sean insisted on helping her even though we'd never even met her," he revealed. "She never speaks of the connection though. Since she prefers that it not be known, we respect that."

Holden could see that his words gave Garret food for thought. He figured it would be a lot easier for Garret to understand his boss if he knew the truth. Plus, it wasn't exactly a secret and since Garret was family now, he deserved to know what he was getting into with the Antaeus clan. He went on to tell his mate about his sisters and brothers. Garret sat sipping his wine, taking in everything Holden told him with a thoughtful expression on his face.

Once the dinner dishes and room service cart were out in the hallway, Holden grabbed Garret by the arm, pulling him in for a hot kiss. "I have a movie for us," he murmured against Garret's mouth.

"Yeah?" Garret's hands cupped his ass and squeezed. Holden could feel his cock stirring. The more Garret played with his ass, the more sensitive it seemingly became.

"Oh, yeah. It's part of the reason I drove you nuts yesterday."

Holden pulled away and went into the bedroom, knowing Garret would follow. Stripping off his clothes he grabbed the remote and turned on the TV and DVD player. The movie started where Holden had left off with it. He looked over at Garret and caught him in the middle of removing his shorts. As the first set of moans filtered from the TV, Garret's head jerked up and his eyes widened in surprise.

"Holden, that's..."

"Porn." Holden finished his mate's shocked statement with a wry smile. "My new motto is never look gift foreplay in the mouth, so don't ask where it came from."

Garret shook his head, his eyes never leaving the TV. "She's not bad looking at all. And would you look at how she—"

"Sucks cock?" Holden said on a laugh. "She's pretty talented."

"I'll say," Garret murmured as he kicked free of his shorts and moved to the bed. "She's extraordinarily good looking for a porn star too."

Holden moved behind his lover, watching as the porn began to excite Garret. "I like redheads. She'd fit pretty well between us, wouldn't you say?" he whispered in Garret's ear.

"Fucking tease."

Garret's words were joking, but they both knew there was an element of truth to them. Holden had wanted to see if the woman turned on Garret as much as she turned him on. Mission accomplished. Now he had plans for the erections the porn had caused. His hands stroked over Garret's lean chest and abs. As his mate leaned back into him, Holden took hold of Garret's thick cock. Stroking Garret in time to the sucks of the woman in the porn soon had them both breathing raggedly.

When Garret spun around, Holden took his mate's mouth in a fierce kiss, passion arcing between them. Like a spark in dry brush, their lust caught fire, turning into a wildfire within minutes, burning out of control and consuming every rational thought they had. As they fell to the mattress, locked in an intense embrace, the remote hit the floor. Both it and the porn were forgotten.

~ * * * ~

The last time Holden had a case of nerves he'd had to face a midterm with a hangover and no sleep. Not suffering from nerves seemed to be a by-product of his natural Antaeus arrogance. None of his siblings got nervous either. Yet, uncharacteristically, the drive back to the city found the inner Holden plagued with nerves. Taking Garret home with him on the eve of the trip to Australia had him on the verge of a major freak out. A thousand questions that he knew were not readily answerable spun inside him. However, he could do nothing but shelve them until answers presented themselves.

By contrast, Garret seemed relaxed sitting beside him in the SUV, but Holden had his doubts about the authenticity of that calm demeanor. They stood on the brink of a new life together with issues to face. Garret surely had some concerns about how they were to make it all work. Holden figured that his new mate's calmness probably had something to do with why he was so successful in the stock market. You needed patience and iron clad nerves to deal with the constant volatility.

Contemplating Garret's steadfast demeanor began to bring down Holden's stress level. If Garret wasn't worried, why should he be? After all, they were in this together. If things went bad, it went bad for both of them. Garret didn't look like he thought that would happen so Holden told his nervous-Nellie core to shut it for now. Somehow, they'd work everything out.

During the long drive, Holden discovered that Garret owned property in England, an upscale loft in London and a country house in Wales. He also found out that the man liked to sky-dive and snorkel, had been a world class swimmer, and had been declared a genius as a small child. He already knew that he liked Garret. As Declan had said, their personalities were compatible. Garret was the best friend Holden had never had.

Maybe that was the reason they were mates, he thought privately. They both held others at an emotional distance. Holden had never had a best friend and had never allowed a woman to get close to him. Garret had closed himself off from others emotionally as a child because most people wanted to use him.

Holden remembered the Asian gardener talking about clearing brush for fire season. Somehow, the man's quiet words had seemed to be about the turmoil inside Holden rather than the gardening work. He realized that those words held true for both himself and Garret. They had both distanced themselves from people in order to not be used or hurt. Now, with respect to the relationship developing between them as men, lovers, and mates, only Holden held back. Garret gave freely of himself and his emotions to his new mate, something that had Holden guilt-ridden.

Despite his best efforts to prevent the wildfire of love and lust that rose in him around Garret, Holden knew he could not escape the fire season of their relationship. It had been too late for him from the moment he'd scented Garret, from the first brush of their lips in that fierce, angry kiss. He'd waited his whole life to find someone who understood him and who he could be comfortable with. The relationship, the mating of his dreams, had arrived and instead of embracing it and being grateful for it, he'd acted the asshole, resisting because his mate was a man and not a woman.

A wave of the most profound emotion Holden had ever felt rose within him as he glanced over at Garret. He owed his lover the full measure of his heart. Now, that he stood on the threshold of opening himself fully to Garret, he had to leave. The timing pissed him off and frustrated him. Garret seemed to take it in stride more easily than he did. He was eager to show Garret how much he had grown to care for him, but now, time was his enemy.

"You're stressing." Garret's words held a hint of amusement.

Holden sighed heavily. "Yeah. And it's not typical of me either," he admitted. "This thing between us, our mating, our relationship, it's new and I don't appreciate having it interrupted by work. The adjustment is difficult enough without a separation tossed into the mix."

One of Garret's dark brows rose in a sardonic expression. "You have such a way with words, Holden. 'The adjustment is difficult enough'? Are you really still adjusting to the fact that I am your mate?" He leaned closer, his hand coming to rest on Holden's jean clad thigh in a light caress. "Your mouth was on my cock only hours ago and you loved it. I think you've adjusted."

Garret's hot breath tickled Holden's neck as his lover leaned over the center console and kissed the side of his throat. They both shuddered as the heat of lust flared instantly between them. Returning to his seat, Garret flashed his gorgeous smile, and Holden saw that his eyes danced with mischief.

"Drive," Garret commanded. "The sooner we arrive at your home, the sooner I can get you naked."

Holden laughed out loud. A strangely carefree feeling came over him. "We're ordering in. I don't want to share you tonight if I have to leave tomorrow afternoon."

When they hit the lowland freeway that fed into the coastal cities, they both grew a little tenser. By the time Holden stopped the SUV at Garret's hotel, he'd decided that he needed to escalate things with his mate when they got home. With a mental sigh, he realized that the condo really was his home, now that he had a mate.

By some silent agreement, Holden waited in the truck while Garret picked up the rest of his things and checked out. While Garret was gone, Holden called his sister-in-law.

"Hello, Holden. Should I guess what you want or should I just let you spit it out," Careen teased him.

Holden made a face even though Sean's wife couldn't see it. "I gather my brother called you," he replied in a mocking tone, knowing very well that Sean shared everything he knew with his mate.

Careen laughed. "He always calls me. He doesn't leave me alone sometimes," she complained. "This time I really didn't mind that he interrupted the laundry. I was very happy to hear your news, Holden. How do you feel?"

"Dazed. Elated. Scared. Happy. Horny." Holden could have gone on longer but he figured those five things covered the majority of his emotions.

There was a definite snicker in Careen's laugh now. "You have a way with words," she snarked.

"So I've been told." Holden grinned, thinking of Garret saying those very words only an hour before.

"Well, mating is hard to do. Your emotions will level off soon. It's tough in the beginning because being horny all the time just throws your brain all out of whack. You can't be logical about anything that has to do with your mate," she told him.

"That's truer than you know," Holden said on a long sigh. "And since when weren't you and Sean not horny all the time? The two of you are the most insanely horny people I know. Nothing on that front has changed that I've seen in the five years you've been together."

Careen giggled. "Okay, I'll concede that. What I really meant was that before you actually mate the urges and the pull inside you makes things worse. After you mate, you level off inside. Your fears disappear and you can really focus on who your mate is. Trying to figure it all out before you mate is not a task for the weak minded."

His sister-in-law's tone grew sharp and Holden knew that her warning was for his own good. "Don't over think it at this stage, Holden. It just is. Mate him and the rest will fall into place. Our ancestors weren't burdened with the cultural claptrap that we are. They found their mates. They mated them. No wondering about compatibility and merging finances and deciding where to live or how many kids to have and whether they loved each other. They just did what their instincts told them to and everything worked itself out." Careen laughed a little. "It still ends up being that way so the stressing is a total waste of time."

Holden stared out the windshield of the truck. Damn. She was right. In spades. "I'll take your advice to heart, Careen," he said gratefully. "This whole having a man for a mate thing threw me, but I think I'm over the worst of my confusion."

A soft sound escaped Careen. "You love him already."

Closing his eyes on a wave of emotion, Holden whispered, "Yes."

"We're lucky to have him in this family. Anyone who can make you sound like that is special." Careen cleared her throat then. "Now, was there something else you wanted?"

Drawing a deep breath and opening his eyes, forcing himself away from the visions in his head of himself and Garret wrapped around each other, loving each other, Holden told his sister-in-law about the penthouse. Luckily, spending his money excited her and it made it easier for him to get past the huge lump in his throat and set aside the emotions that threatened his composure.

By the time Garret returned pulling a large suitcase behind him, Holden had given Careen carte blanche on the condo. Well, other than the fact that she needed to run some things by Garret too. Holden had no worries that between Garret and Careen, he would be returning to a real home, not a bachelor pad.

Walking into the penthouse with Garret had Holden's heart pounding as if he'd run a marathon. He watched in silence as his mate went to the wall of glass that overlooked the coastline. For a long moment, Garret stood there, hands on his hips staring first north then south. Finally, he turned and Holden held his breath.

"It's spectacular." Garret sighed, his chest expanding his t-shirt. Holden couldn't look away from him. The pleasure and love in those green irises drew him like a lodestone. "I couldn't have chosen anything more perfect. The view is like flying."

Relief flooded Holden. "That's why I wanted it. I love to fly, but I work a lot and rarely get the chance. This room is the next best thing to being naked in the air with the wind on my scales. Why do you think the couch faces the windows instead of the TV?"

Garret walked over to him. Holding his mate's gaze, Holden felt him slide one hand up his arm to grasp his bicep. Fire licked along every nerve ending in Holden's body. This was his mate, his home—*their* home—and he wanted to show Garret just how committed he was to the relationship. Leaning closer, his chest brushing Garret's, Holden captured his lover's mouth in a passionate kiss.

Reaching down, he ran his hands over Garret's hips and thighs, stroking over his tight buttocks before cupping them. He pressed Garret toward him, their hips banging together. Beneath his jeans, Holden's cock surged into a full blown erection. Hands on Garret's ass, he pushed his lover against his hard body, rubbing against him and feeling the hot rush of his response. Ripping at Garret's clothes, a single thought dominated Holden's actions.

Mate me!

The shared thought fueled the haste with which they removed their clothes. Once naked, Holden maneuvered them toward the glass doors. With a muffled growl, Garret pulled away and reached for his suitcase. Holden grabbed his arm, dragging him back against his naked chest. They kissed again, Holden's damp lips sliding across Garret's. Flicking his tongue against his mate's, Holden broke the kiss and reached for his jacket, his hand emerging from the pocket with a tube of lube.

Garret shivered, the pupils of his eyes elongating as they stepped out to the wide balcony. Holden nipped at his mate's jaw line, feeling his dragon fangs extending inside his mouth. The soft afternoon breeze caressed Holden's skin as Garret touched him, palms stroking over the slabs of muscle on his chest and abdomen. By the time Garret's fist closed around Holden's straining erection, both of them had begun to tremble.

Now, Garret. I want to mate you now.

No foreplay? Garret teased.

Fuck! The whole goddamned drive down the mountain was foreplay. I want to mate you. I don't want to wait anymore. I know who you are. I know who I am. I know we belong together. Please don't tell me no.

Garret's eyes glowed a deep dark green as smoke trailed from his nostrils. *I can't say no. I want this as much as you do. It's only fitting we do this here, in our home, yet out in the open air.*

Holden kissed his mate, taking his time, letting their tongues tangle with growing heat. *I'm going to fuck you and bathe you in my fire until every part of you belongs to me.*

Possessive.

Gods, yes!

Garret's eyes filled with emotion. Holden trembled a little as he turned his lover around, pressing him against the wall that ringed the balcony. Bent at the waist, Garret glanced over his shoulder at Holden. Ripping the cap off the tube of lube, Holden squirted it into his hand. First he slid his palm against his cock, his fingers curling over it, making sure it was slick. Another squirt from the tube slathered his fingers and he pressed Garret's knees apart, opening him.

Holden's fingers slipped over Garret's anus and his lover shivered in reaction, moaning loudly.

"No one will see. No one will hear. It's just you and me up here, Garret," Holden murmured as his fingers stroked the entrance to Garret's dark hole. "No other condos on this floor. No other buildings this height on this block. We're all alone up here and I am going to fuck you so good you will scream my name to the clouds."

"Do it," Garret panted harshly. "Put your cock in me, Holden."

Holden smiled, his fingers pressing for entrance. He worked the lube into Garret, ignoring his lover's moans of delight. Pulling his fingers free, he replaced them with his cock, the head pressing steadily against Garret's sensitive flesh. Placing one hand on Garret's clan mark, Holden thrust into his mate, hearing the satisfied growl of his dragon inside his head.

Smoke poured from Garret as he pushed back against Holden's hips. Knowing that he would be bathing Garret in his fire within minutes, a primeval sense of possession, almost of ownership, came over Holden. This was *his* mate, *his* lover, *his man* and no one else would ever possess him.

As he leaned over Garret's back, the ridges of his lower abdomen rubbed Garret's clan mark. His tongue snaked out to tease the lobe of his lover's ear as he whispered, "You. Are. Mine." Each word was punctuated with a thrust that pressed Garret into the low wall.

His hands absorbed the shudders that racked Garret's lean body. He dug his fingers into his lover's muscles, feeling them flex as Garret's orgasm neared. With one hand he stroked Garret's thigh then reached for his cock. Feeling his own orgasm coming almost too soon, Holden stroked the thick length of Garret's cock, his fingers gliding over the flesh easily because of the lube and pre-cum. Garret groaned as Holden continued to pump his cock into Garret's tight channel.

Nuzzling the thick muscle between Garret's shoulder and neck, Holden's curved dragon fangs scraped Garret's collarbone. Pleasure poured into him as Garret's mind opened, letting him feel and hear every emotion and sensation that racked Garret's body. He stroked his lover's cock with deliberate movements, inciting him to come. The tight heated passage that cradled his cock began to rhythmically clutch his flesh.

Yeah, baby. Come for me, Garret. Can you feel what you do to me? I'm going to come and it's just for you. Only you...

Harder, Holden. Fuck me harder. I can't get enough of you!

Holden's hand squeezed and slid along the thickness of Garret's straining erection. He pressed harder against his lover, feeling the pre-orgasmic tremors that shook Garret's frame. Scraping his fangs along Garret's flesh, he breathed in his spearmint scent, the scent that seemed to fill the air around them. A buzz began in his balls, spreading to his groin followed by an intense heat that rose in his body.

With a dragon roar, Holden's orgasm exploded as he thrust into Garret. Shaking, he felt Garret's cock jerk in his grasp. As his lover's cock began pumping out cum, Holden pressed his face to the crook of Garret's neck. Swiftly, he struck, his fangs sinking deep into Garret's flesh.

Crying out, Garret turned his head as Holden raised his face, blood dripping from his fangs. Garret slashed at Holden's shoulder his own fangs grabbing onto muscle and bone. With a groan, he released Holden only to find his mouth taken in a kiss so filled with passion his knees grew weak. The blood on their fangs mingled in their mouths as their tongues twisted together. With a flash of bright white light, they each released their dragonfire.

Intense heat enveloped them, sending a cloud of smoke into the air. Garret went rigid beneath Holden and for long moments they stood frozen as dragonfire raced through their bodies. Finally, their orgasms faded, tumescent flesh became soft again, and the smell of brimstone left the air.

Holden kissed Garret on the back of the neck. As he pulled away from his mate, he saw the dark lines of a clan mark swirling up from the one Garret had in the small of his back. On his own back he felt a prickle and knew his mark was changing too. Soon the marks would be identical. After licking up the drops of blood on Garret's shoulder and making sure that the wound had begun to close, Holden took a step backward catching Garret's hand.

"We are mated now. You are my present and my future," he said softly, gazing into Garret's bright green eyes.

"As you're my mate now. You are my forever."

They came together in a kiss so filled with emotion that Holden thought he would burst. Happiness spilled through him and a sense of being complete settled in his heart.

"I didn't think the day would ever come that I would have a mate, let alone one who understands me, understands my work and my devotion to my family." His eyes never left Garret's as he spoke the words in his heart. "Someone who can be my partner, my lover, and my best friend. I can't believe I found you, Garret."

His mate chuckled, his emerald eyes sparkling with happiness. "You didn't. Alfred did."

Holden tugged on Garret's hand and led him into the condo. "We'll send him a thank you gift. Some new golf clubs or something," Holden said with a laugh. "We owe him."

"I think you're right. I know I'm feeling very grateful to Alfred Stone right now," Garret agreed. He looked Holden up and down, his gaze assessing. "Did you say you had a Jacuzzi tub?"

With a nod, Holden led the way to the bathroom. Garret's eyes gleamed. "I always wanted to see if my dragonfire would make the water boil. Care to try out my theory? I know you like being bathed in my fire," he teased.

"We have all night to test the waters of our mating." Holden spoke the bad joke while grinning wickedly. "No reason not to start here."

He turned on the faucet and looked over his shoulder at Garret, his emotions suddenly raw and close to the surface as he stared at the man he would share his life with. Swallowing hard to push back the lump that had formed in his throat, he said, "I know the past few days have been tough. I know my vacillations and confusion made everything more complicated than it should have been. But Garret, I cannot deny what I feel in the very marrow of my bones..."

Garret went very still, his gaze holding Holden's steadily. "You don't have to..."

Holden shook his head, cutting off Garret's words. "I *do* have to. I *need* to tell you that I love you, Garret Renquist."

His quiet confession turned Garret's face into an expression of such sheer joy that Holden's heart tumbled in his chest. "I love you too, Holden."

The rush of emotion he felt from his mate overwhelmed him. "Then let's see if we can make the water boil," he said gruffly, turning off the taps.

As he turned back to Garret, his mate caught him by the chin and pulled his face close. "You make my temperature rise. You make me so hot, if I wasn't a dragon, I'd have melted long ago," he whispered fiercely.

Their mouths crushed together and they both moaned at the exquisite sensations that rocked their bodies. Holden pulled back, his thumb rubbing over Garret's wet lower lip. "Come on, lover. Our science experiment awaits," he said in a low voice filled with emotion. "We have all night and half the day tomorrow to talk about love. I'm going to make love to you in this tub. Then again in my bed—our bed—as long as you can take it. I'm making memories so that while I'm gone, I'll be able to think of you lying naked in my bed, wrapped in my scent."

Garret stepped into the tub. "You know, I might have been joking before, but I'm not now," he replied in a voice filled with desire. "You really do have a way with words, Holden Antaeus."

~ * * * ~

Holden's emotions felt raw and exposed as he stood beside the limo, knowing that both his brother Declan and Garret's boss Emily were inside. At the same time, he just didn't care. He and Garret belonged together and he didn't give a shit who knew it. Garret stepped toward him, pressing him against the side of the limo. They touched from breast bone to thighs, every muscle and sinew straining. Holden's body screamed for Garret's, wanting only to be naked, to take his mate.

Garret's beard roughened jaw scraped Holden's as they kissed with a feverish frenzy. Hands stroked and tugged, slipping under shirts, into waistbands. Hips rubbed, teasing already sensitive engorged cocks separated by the annoying layers of their clothes.

Holden moaned. "They're... watching... us," he panted as he licked Garret's lips.

The wet smacking of their kisses and licking at each other's mouths filled the air around them. "No... they're not," Garret replied, his fingers teasing the waistband of Holden's boxer briefs.

With a shudder at the touch of flesh on flesh, Holden rubbed his hips against Garret's. "Everyone else on the street is looking," he groaned, then flicked his tongue along Garret's, sliding it into his lover's mouth, letting the teasing kiss push him to the point where he was about to tell his brother he'd take a later flight.

A shrill screech forced their mouths to part as they both turned to see a tall, dark haired woman in a designer dress stalking toward them across the sidewalk.

Holden's stomach clenched and anger shot through him. "What are you doing here, Gina?" he asked harshly.

The brunette stopped in front of them, her chest heaving, her beautiful face set in an expression of outrage. "I came to see you. To talk to you about the bracelet you sent me and ask you why you broke up with me," she replied in an angry voice. Her dark eyes flashed. "But I can see now why you did."

"Gina, if you'll give me a moment I can explain," Holden said in an even voice, hoping to placate her enough that she'd shut up and go the fuck away.

Garret's body stiffened against him and Holden knew that he had somehow stepped into deep waters.

"I don't need an explanation from you, Holden Antaeus. I have eyes. I can see quite clearly that you dumped me because you're a fag!" she retorted in a scathing voice, her eyes sweeping over them with a dismissive glare.

Every muscle in Garret's body turned to stone. Holden could feel it quite clearly since that body still pinned him against the side of the limo. Frustration and anger boiled over inside him.

"Gina, I'm not gay. Garret is..."

"Fuck you!" she screamed, her face contorting into a mask of fury. "You dumped me for a...a...little faggot! You're nothing but a cocksucker, Holden!" She took two steps backward. "How many years did you lie to yourself, pretending you were straight when you were fucking women's asses? Did you fantasize that I was *him* when you fucked *my* ass? Is that how you managed the lie?"

Holden shook with rage. He pushed Garret aside with a growl and grabbed Gina by the arm. "You don't know what the fuck you're talking about, Gina. I broke up with you because the only thing you ever cared about was my damned money. I wasn't ever going to marry you and you knew it," he snarled, dragging her down the sidewalk toward a BMW convertible parked behind the limo. "You're not my mate. *He* is! And if you ever come around here again, I'll call building security *and* the cops."

Gina glared around him at Garret who stood frozen on the sidewalk, his body stiff as a board. "Go on back to your butt buddy. I don't want you anymore. I prefer to be with a real man not some asshole who spouts 'gay for you' mate bullshit and can't even admit he's a fag," she said in a venomous tone. "Have a nice cock sucking life, Holden!"

Jerking her arm from his hold, she got in the BMW and slammed the door, gunning the engine. Holden stood shaking on the curb as she pulled away, tires smoking. When he looked up, he saw Declan standing beside the limo with the door open and a worried expression on his face.

"I'm coming," he said grimly to his brother as he walked toward Garret.

He reached out and touched the side of Garret's face, but his mate stiffened and turned away. "Garret?" His hand tried to catch his lover's. Garret backed away.

"I'll speak to you in a day or two." The clipped British accent was completely formal and panic began to bubble in his veins.

"Garret, I'm sorry." Holden wasn't sure what to do or say to make up for the horrendous scene that had just occurred.

His mate nodded briefly, but his face remained impassive. "I am too."

Turning on his heel, Garret went into the high rise, leaving Holden standing shattered on the sidewalk in front of the limo.

"Holden. Let's go." The sympathetic tones of Declan's voice were soft but firm. "He'll get over his anger soon enough. We have a plane to catch."

Holden's heart screamed at him to just blow off the damned trip and follow Garret back up the penthouse. His mate's thoughts were shut off to him and Holden knew that Garret was beyond pissed. He couldn't even pinpoint what exactly had gotten to Garret. He just knew the man he loved was upset, angry, and disappointed in him. Holden wanted to run after him and throw his arms around him, kiss him and coax him into a better humor.

"Holden!"

This time Declan's voice thundered. With a sinking heart, Holden turned away from the high-rise and walked toward his brother. Declan threw his arm around Holden's shoulders, giving him a brief squeeze.

"You'll sort it out. He loves you."

Declan's soft words filled Holden's ears as he got in the limo. Emily looked at him with huge sad eyes. Holden blinked, startled. He'd never seen her without her icy composure before. Her hazel eyes were filled with tears and her lips trembled with emotion.

"Make it right, Holden," she whispered as Declan got in and the limo pulled away. "You can't lose your mate. The pain is...indescribable." She rubbed her breast bone unconsciously and with a dawning sense of horror, Holden realized she knew what she was talking about. "Do whatever it takes to make things right between you. You both deserve to be happy like Sean and Careen. Not like me and..." She broke off and dipped her head, wiping at her eyes. "Not like me," she finished gruffly and turned away from him to stare out the window.

Holden's eyes met his brother's. They were sympathetic and filled with pain too. "She's right. You have to make it up to him." Declan's warm hand squeezed his knee briefly. "I know you'll figure out a way to get past this. He loves you and you love him. All the screaming harpies in the world can't change that."

They rode the rest of the way to the airport in silence punctuated occasionally by the softest of sniffles from Emily. Holden knew that Garret's anger wasn't so much about Gina as it was about Holden's words and actions. He'd disappointed his new mate somehow and he wasn't sure which of his actions or words had done the deed.

Along his spine his clan mark writhed. He could feel the heat of it as it contorted itself into a new shape because of his mating. He wanted to talk to Garret, but his mate's thoughts were very firmly closed off from him. As the corporate jet's tail and wings came into view, Holden's stomach sank. His dragon bitched and hissed and roared within him at being separated from Garret so soon. The roiling in his stomach, and in his soul, made him feel as if he was about to throw up.

One glance at Emily, huddled in the corner of the limo, limp with misery, made him realize that he would never survive without Garret. He would work like a fiend to finish what Declan needed from him. Eating and sleeping meant nothing to him if it added to the hours and days of separation. The sooner he finished with the takeover, the sooner he could go home and fix his life.

Chapter Eleven

Garret walked through the next ten days like a zombie. If he didn't fill each moment with work until he fell asleep exhausted, his brain conjured up the sound of Holden's voice protesting, "I'm not gay!"

The words were true so Garret wasn't sure exactly why they disappointed him so. Maybe it was because Holden's first words were not "He's my mate!" For Garret, the whole scene had been one huge painful blot on his relationship with Holden. He'd been flying so damn high too, newly mated, feeling his clan mark twisting and changing until it writhed up his spine making him want to rip off his shirt and show the world who he belonged to. And who belonged to him.

In his heart, regardless of anything Holden might have said to his ex-girlfriend, Garret knew that they belonged to each other. He knew that Holden felt the same. If Holden hadn't felt the emotion in his heart, he would never have bathed Garret in his dragonfire. Perhaps it was the newness of their mating that had made the confrontation with Gina sting so badly. The instant he'd walked away from Holden, Garret had felt his mate's pain. It had been all he could do to walk into the building and get in the elevator. He'd wanted to run back to Holden and kiss him and fuck him into submission. He'd been filled with the urge to prove to Holden how special their relationship was.

Each day that Holden was gone felt like a nail in Garret's coffin. At night, in Holden's bed, he tossed and turned, his body aching for his mate. Every day at Antaeus International seemed tenser than the last. Stressful didn't even cover it when it came to work. Without Emily there to smooth his transition into the company and without Holden to help him acclimatize, everything seemed to take longer to do and whatever could go wrong did.

To Garret's surprise, Sean had been helpful and supportive. One afternoon, he'd shown up in Garret's new office, dressed for golf, with Alfred Stone and Marius Granville flanking him. All three men had praised his work and stroked his ego. He'd gone home feeling much better about what he did at Antaeus International.

Still, Holden's thoughts didn't leak out to him and each day that went by without contact made his heart heavier. His stiff British upper lip wouldn't let him admit that he yearned for his mate with every breath he took. A couple of times, he'd tentatively tried to reach out to Holden but caught himself before he could interrupt his lover's work or sleep. Never having had a mate before and never having been on the wrong side of a disagreement that wasn't exactly a disagreement, Garret didn't know how to handle what had happened between them the afternoon that Holden left for Australia.

He spoke with Emily three times in the ten days they'd been gone. Each time she'd seemed more lackluster and inattentive than the last. Garret felt the way she sounded.

Careen had taken him to lunch both days on the weekend and dragged him around to a lot of stores asking him his opinion on a bunch of stuff he didn't much care about. During the week, on the nights he hadn't worked late, she and Sean had taken him to dinner. He'd been dragged to an industry event as well where he'd met all of the Granvilles from Granville Cemetery and Alfred's brother, Austin, too. Afterward, he'd had a little too much to drink with Vahid and Brian Dumont.

He'd been shocked at Vahid's drinking, but Brian told him Vahid had been under a lot of stress lately and Sean had ordered him to take a vacation. Brian worked closely with Holden and held a law degree as well. He was just waiting for Declan's call to come take Holden's place. As they drank, he told Garret he was surprised he hadn't yet received the notice. Apparently, Holden and Declan usually worked much quicker. Either the Australian takeover was a nasty bitch on wheels or they were biding their time over it.

Any way that Garret looked at it, it seemed his mate wouldn't be coming home any time soon. So it was with a profound sense of shock that he heard the key turn in the lock at 3 o'clock in the morning on the eleventh day of their separation. Part of him wanted to jump up and run to greet Holden. Before he could decide, Holden's shadow appeared in the open bedroom doorway.

"I'm so fucking sorry."

The words were croaked out in a hoarse whisper filled with more pain than Garret had ever heard in anyone's voice before. He turned over onto his back and rose up on his elbows. "Why didn't you call to tell me you were coming home?" he asked, in a low tone.

Holden took two shaky steps into the room. "I'm sorry, Garret. Everything I said. Everything I did came out wrong that morning. Whatever pissed you off, I didn't mean it." A pleading note entered Holden's voice. "Please, Garret. I'm not even sure which thing hurt you and it's been tearing me up inside to the point that I'm useless to Declan and the company. I spent every moment that I was there wishing I was home with you."

A lump formed in Garret's throat. Ten days later, he wasn't sure either what had upset him so. All he knew was that he'd missed Holden fiercely. He reached over and threw back the covers, inviting Holden in.

With a low sound that seemed to come from the depths of his chest, Holden stumbled to the side of the bed, pulling his clothes off.

When he slid between the sheets, his naked thigh brushing Garret's, electricity crackled between them. However, instead of sexual heat flaring instantly, Garret's heart soared in a way it never had before. Holden pressed against him, his arms wrapping tightly around Garret as they sat on the mattress.

Feeling Holden's nuzzles on the curve of his neck below his ear, Garret's heart contracted painfully. With a rush, their minds opened and their thoughts mingled. Garret hugged Holden in a tight embrace, feeling how overcome by emotion his mate was.

Oh, gods. I missed you so much. I spent the whole time stressing over us.

I missed you too, Holden. I'm sorry I was so angry. I'm not even sure now what exactly set me off.

I was wrong. I shouldn't have said anything to her. I should have just told her it was none of her business and sent her away. Nothing is more important to me than you. Nothing. Not Antaeus International. Not my brothers or my sisters. Only this.

Holden's arms tightened around Garret as their mouths met. They both moaned at the pleasure that swept over them. At first, their kisses were short and sweet, damp lips clinging while their hearts conveyed their feelings to each other. Garret traced the seam of Holden's lips with the tip of his tongue. When Holden's mouth opened, Garret's tongue swept inside. Their kisses had an edge of desperation in them from the long days of their separation. Holden sucked on Garret's tongue as his hands stroked the clan mark that now swept from his lower back up between his shoulder blades, two entwined dragons, both black but one with an emerald in its mouth. Without looking, Garret knew that Holden's mark now matched his.

A groan came from their mashed together lips, but Garret wasn't sure if it was his groan or Holden's.

I'm so glad you're home. I love you, Holden.

Holden pressed closer, his body tight against Garret's. *I love you too, Garret. I don't think I can even convey how much I love you.*

Garret felt his mate shaking with a combination of exhaustion and an excess of emotion. He slid down into the bed, cradling Holden to him and tugging at the sheet with one hand. A heavy sigh escaped Holden as he relaxed, his body going limp.

So tired.

Sleep, love. I'll be right here with you. I'm never going to let you go, you know.

Good. Cause I need you, Garret.

Within moments, Holden fell into a deep sleep. Garret held him, nuzzling his soft inky hair until he too fell asleep.

~ * * * ~

Garret awoke to the feel of hands stroking his cock. He smiled without opening his eyes. Holden was there and all was right with his world.

"Did you buy a car yet?"

"No," he replied, still not opening his eyes. "I couldn't bear to. Your car smells like you.'

Holden's hand stroked him with a twisting motion that sent pleasure shooting through his veins. He sighed, his hips arching into his mate's touch.

"Fireball time," Holden teased.

Now, Garret's eyes opened. Golden irises with dark elongated pupils stared down at him. "You want to kiss me then?"

Holden grinned. "I always want to kiss you, touch you, lick you, fuck you."

Garret raised one brow as he rolled over, sitting up. "That's a nice little sex rhyme."

"Isn't it? It's my new mantra."

Garret could see that his mate was supremely happy. He had to admit, he was too. Chuckling, they swallowed fireballs and fell into each other's arms, kicking the covers to the floor and rolling all the over bed as their mouths met in a passionate kiss. Garret nipped at Holden's lower lip and growled. Holden's hands teased the crease of Garret's ass, making him shudder. Their hips pressed together, the hard ridges of their cocks rubbing against each other.

Pre-cum leaked copiously from their cocks, wetting their abs and making the friction feel delicious. Panting, Holden's gaze caught and held Garret's as their lips parted.

"Fuck me, Garret. I want to feel you inside me. I want to know what you feel when I'm deep inside you and coming so hard I think my brains are going into shock."

The words were delivered in a voice that shook with a combination of fear and excitement. Garret completely understood the level of trust and commitment Holden had just handed him and it made his heart soar.

He stroked his hands over Holden's face, tracing the beloved angles and planes. "I've wanted to make love to you for so long," he murmured. "I can't wait to move in you and watch the pleasure streak across your face."

"Then do it." Holden's expression was fierce, filled with more lust than Garret had ever seen him express before. "Get the lube."

Garret reached into the drawer of the nightstand and emerged with a new tube. He stroked his palm over Holden's pecs. "We don't have to do this today," he said softly. "We can build up to it."

Holden grabbed Garret's chin, kissing him hard on the mouth. "No. I love you. I need to feel like I belong to you."

A chuckle rose from Garret's chest. "You don't feel like you belong to me now?" he asked teasingly, his hand stroking Holden's cock. "This is mine. Your cock. Your thoughts. Your heart. And your ass, although I've barely stuck a finger in it."

Holden choked on a laugh. "Did you know that you have a way with words too?"

Garret nodded, noticing that there were spots of color high on Holden's tanned cheekbones. That told Garret that his mate's comfort level wasn't quite where it should be. Garret would bet that Holden was a lot more virgin than most men. He had a sense that even Holden's female partners hadn't invaded his dark hole. However, the fact that Holden was now open to anything between the two of them spoke volumes about how far he had come in his acceptance that love and mating was people specific not gender specific.

Still, Garret knew how sensitive that area of Holden's body was. He'd stroked it enough times while sucking Holden's cock to know that it was a major erogenous zone for his mate. It did make him curious to know why Holden had never indulged in anal play before.

"Maybe I was saving myself for you."

For a moment, Garret was silent. His startled eyes met Holden's. The black dragon's face was a study in amusement. Then a huge laugh roared up out of Garret. He leaned in and kissed Holden, flicking his tongue over his mate's sensitive lips.

"I can't imagine belonging to anyone else. You complete me, Holden," he murmured, his mouth still curved in a smile even as he kissed his mate.

"You say that now. The first time we share a woman you'll be pissed that I'm such a selfish bastard." The teasing light in Holden's eyes sent waves of emotion crashing through Garret.

"I may get angry with you, but I will never love anyone the way I love you." Garret's words were spoken with a quiet ferocity that found an answering fire in his mate's eyes.

"Just fuck me, Garret," Holden said on a soft breath, his voice shaking with emotion.

Garret sprawled atop his lover, his hands caressing every inch of Holden's smooth skin. He nuzzled Holden's throat then took his mouth in a deep kiss. Their tongues tangled, stroking and teasing.

I could do that to your ass. Wriggle my tongue just like that.

Holden's eyes blazed up at him. *Another time. I need you to fuck me and kiss me. No way is your tongue going from my ass to my mouth.*

Garret snickered softly. *Fireball.*

Maybe another time, Holden insisted. *Right now, there's only so much new stuff I can take.*

You'll take me...

And I'm sure I'll love it.

It will hurt, Holden, Garret warned, his fingers digging into his mate's hip. *I'm not small, and you've never been stretched.*

Holden's hands caressed the back of Garret's head. *I want all of you. I already know it won't be all pleasure, but I need this. I need you. Just fuck me already.*

Garret broke their kiss, his chest heaving as he rose to his knees, straddling Holden's hips. "Turn over."

Slowly, Holden rolled to his belly. Garret's thighs and knees quivered with the effort to remain still as his mate pushed up on his knees enough to elevate his hips and buttocks. With his breathing harsh even to his own ears, Garret stroked his hand over the smooth muscular curve of Holden's right ass cheek. His dragon growled, urging him to take Holden. Garret knew he had to go slow. He wanted the experience to be something his mate would want repeated often.

Garret's eyes caressed the masculine curves of Holden's body. All those rippling muscles were his to touch and lick forever. A shudder of pleasure went through him and his cock twitched. Holden's fierce beauty held him enthralled. One hand skated over his lover's hip to grasp his straining cock. A moan broke from Holden and his back bowed. Leaning over him, Garret's tongue swirled along his mate's clan mark. Impossibly, he felt Holden's cock surge and thicken in his grip.

Licking his way down the clan mark from shoulder blades to the small of Holden's back, Garret felt his lover's desire rising rapidly. Sitting back on his haunches, he pressed Holden's hips higher, one hand kneading the black dragon's firm buttocks as the other continued to stroke his cock. Letting his fingers trace the crease between the globes, his touch light and teasing, Garret carefully gauged the level of Holden's excitement. When he realized that his mate was nearly mindless with lust, he reluctantly let go of his cock and reached for the lube.

Generous amounts of the slick liquid poured into Garret's palm. He shivered, knowing what the lube was for, what it meant. His cock ached in a way that pushed his control to the edge. With trembling hands, he pressed Holden's buttocks apart and stroked his wet fingers over the puckered entrance. He heard Holden's breath hiss, but staring at the place where he would soon put his cock had him on a single-minded mission. Again, he stroked his fingers over Holden's anus, rubbing copious amounts of lube in and around it.

A long shuddering moan escaped Holden as Garret pressed a finger past the tight, virgin ring of muscles. Gently, Garret pressed his finger into the wet, resistant hole. The heat of Holden's channel surrounding his finger almost made him come. Panting loudly, sweat breaking out at his hairline, Garret slowly fucked Holden with his finger. When Holden began to thrust back onto the digit, Garret squirted more lube and pressed a second finger into his lover.

"Ohhhhh!" Holden's moans grew loud and uncontrolled as Garret fucked him with two fingers.

Do you like that, baby?

Oh, gods, Garret. You never told me it would feel like this.

I'm not hurting you, am I?

No, no. Garret, I need more. Fuck me!

The lust filled thoughts of his mate made Garret tremble. He pulled his fingers from Holden's body and stroked lube thickly over his cock.

Breathe, Holden. Just concentrate on your breathing, he told his mate as he pressed the head of his cock to Holden's anus. He rubbed the crown against Holden's sensitive flesh and felt a shudder go though him. *You want this, don't you? You want my cock in your ass, filling you.*

Yes! Damn you, Garret! Stop teasing me and fuck me already! How many times do I have to beg?

Garret's hand stroked over Holden's clan mark and he felt his mate writhe with lust, his back bowing, his hips thrusting backward. Pressing forward, his cock felt the stiff resistance of Holden's virgin hole.

Breathe, baby. Just breathe and give it up to me. He pushed relentlessly at Holden's anus, feeling his lover quiver beneath the onslaught. *Don't hold your breath! It will hurt worse. Just breathe...*

With a firm thrust, his thick cock head burst through the tight sphincter muscles. Beneath him, Holden cried out, and then froze. Garret stroked the clan mark with a shaking hand. "Holden? Tell me you're okay," he commanded, his voice wobbling slightly.

"It burns," Holden panted. "But it's going away. Oh, gods, Garret. You're inside me..."

The awed tone in his lover's voice catered directly to Garret's possessiveness. He stroked the clan mark with a deliberately sensuous touch as he pressed his cock a little further into Holden's heated channel. Taking his time, stopping after each press inward, he finally felt his balls slap up against his mate's. After giving Holden a few moments to get used to the thick length of cock inside him, Garret began to move. He knew that his first stroke had to burn with pain. He squirted more lube on his cock and Holden's ass and pressed in again. Holden moaned.

Breathe, baby. Push against the stroke and the burn will ease. Plus, it feels better when you do that. You'll feel my cock hit your prostate and you'll think lightning struck your dick.

I'm trying, Garret. It feels amazing.

Garret dropped a kiss on Holden's clan mark. *You're mine. I'm so deep inside you and you are all mine, Holden.*

Another shudder went through Holden and feeling that the pain had eased in his lover's tight channel, Garret began to fuck him with short, easy strokes. He'd never fucked anyone so tight or so hot before. Holden' body pressed back against his eagerly. As his strokes began to come harder, Holden began to tremble and moan loudly. Garret knew he'd begun to hit Holden's prostate with the harder, longer strokes. The pleasure that rocketed through his lover's body went through his as well.

Reaching around Holden's hip, he stroked his mate's stiff cock. Fondling Holden's balls, he felt them tightening, pulling closer to his body, and knew his mate was close to orgasm. Garret resumed stroking Holden's cock. He fucked his mate harder, his hips slapping against Holden's ass. Incoherent moans filled the room and Garret couldn't tell if they were his or Holden's.

Garret! Oh, gods, fuck me harder. I'm going to come!

The wonder that Holden felt at being possessed by his mate leaked straight into Garret's head. He knew everything Holden felt from the pain to the intense pleasure to the love that swelled within him at the feel of Garret's cock moving inside him.

Garret pulled Holden up off his arms, bending his body back until his mate was cradled in his arms. Holden turned his head and their lips met. Tongues twisting around each other, Garret's hand tightly stroking Holden's cock, his own cock buried deep in Holden's hot ass, their minds completely open to each other's thoughts and feelings with not a single thing held back. The fierceness of their orgasms came over them in that moment of pure connection. It exploded with a heat and intensity that surpassed their mating.

Garret!

Holden!

As far as Garret was concerned, there really weren't words to describe how it felt when his cock unleashed it's cum inside Holden for the first time. Holden's cock pumped out a steady stream of cum all over his hand and the wet warmth told Garret how much pleasure his mate had derived from being fucked. They collapsed on the mattress, rolling to their sides away from the splatter of cum on the sheets. Garret's cock slipped from Holden's heated, spasming channel. He buried his face in the curve of Holden's shoulder, trailing kisses along his lover's skin.

They lay quietly for a long time, occasionally kissing softly and caressing each other. Finally, Garret sighed. "We should clean up," he murmured in a regretful tone.

"Why?" Holden replied with a low chuckle. "Who cares if we're lying here in a puddle of cum?"

"Ugh." Garret grimaced. "I don't want to move. I love just lying here with you in my arms, but the puddle of cum is just not conducive to romantic thoughts."

Holden twisted around until they were face to face. "Do you feel romantic about me? I mean, we're men. Do men feel like that about each other?" he asked curiously.

Garret brushed back the wayward lock of black hair that fell over Holden's brow. "I feel that way about you. You're my mate. I think I'm supposed to feel that way about you," he said with quiet honesty. "I know that I love you with every cell and atom of my body. I know that my soul feels whole and complete now. My life feels richer and worth living now."

Holden's amber eyes widened a little. "You're really very eloquent for a bean counter, did you know that?" he murmured, his mouth turning up at the corner in a wry smile.

"I'm not a bean counter."

At Garret's words, Holden kissed him, giving him a quick tongue rub. Then he smiled. "No. You're not a bean counter. You're my mate. My love. You are the reason for each breath that I draw, each beat of my heart..."

Holden's words were spoken with a soft intensity that had Garret's heart pounding. When Holden took his hand and pressed it to his chest so that Garret could his feel his heart pounding too, the most amazing sense of security and freedom came over Garret.

"... each throb of my cock..."

Garret blinked in surprise and Holden laughed. "If I'm honest I'd say each throb of my ass too," he admitted. "You're big."

"I didn't hurt you, did I?" Garret frowned.

"Nah. I'm okay. It was the most amazing sexual experience of my life though." Holden sighed, his face falling into relaxed lines. "I've learned so much from you, Garret. I know more about being a dragon now than I ever did before. I understand that what is between us is not about gender or sexuality. It's about love and mating and being happy. I've never had a best friend before and now I not only have one, but he knows everything there is to know about me and his very presence fills me with joy."

Garret smiled. "What did you say about men being romantic with men?" His brows rose. "I'd say you just did a damned fine job of it, Holden Antaeus."

"That's because I have it on good authority that I have a way with words, Garret Renquist."

Holden pushed Garret onto his back and got up, heading into the bathroom. He returned with washcloths and they cleaned each other, making jokes about fireballs. Afterward, Holden pushed Garret onto his back again and stretched out on top of him. Garret could feel both their cocks stirring as he stroked his hands down Holden's clan mark. Inside, his dragon practically purred with pleasure. It was funny how love tamed the beasts inside them, he thought.

Not funny at all, bean counter. This is the way life is meant to be.

Really? How about you show me what your tongue has learned since I met you, Mr. Tennis Trophies.

It will forever be my very great pleasure to show you just how much I love you.

Garret cupped his hands around Holden's handsome face. *I didn't think there was this much happiness in the world, let alone for me. Thank you, Holden.*

One of Holden's dark brows quirked up. *You're thanking me now? Before I've put my mouth on your cock?*

One can never be too thankful or too grateful. I love you, Holden. Garret pressed a quick kiss to Holden's mouth. *Now, where was it that you said you were going to put your mouth?*

Holden laughed out loud, the sound filled with happiness. *Now, that fire season is over and there's no longer any distance between us... I'm going to put my mouth to good use setting fire to your lust.*

That's one wildfire I'll never want to die out.

Garret grinned as Holden shifted over him, facing his cock.

Good. Now, can we get on with lesson number two in soixante neuf?

I don't understand how you passed the bar when you can't learn a lesson the first time around.

Holden's hands stroked down Garret's thighs before closing around his cock. *I was teacher's pet.*

Garret sucked in a breath as Holden's mouth began to lick his growing erection. *I can see why.*

Garret. Get busy.

The arrogant thought made Garret smile. *You and that thing with words again.*

Holden chuckled out loud. *Suck me.*

Obediently, Garret sucked Holden's cock into his mouth as lust spread through them like a wildfire and happiness filled their hearts.

Epilogue

Alfred Stone stared into the fire and sipped his brandy. His head ached from all the conversations he'd had to listen to that afternoon. Usually, he could control himself much better and not let too many people in at a time. However, he'd been distracted lately and his concentration was a casualty of it.

Warm hands curved around his neck, massaging the tense muscles. "You need to relax, Al. You work too hard." The soft voice held a sardonic note and Alfred knew the speaker meant that touch of sarcasm. Ash didn't have the most optimistic outlook on life. A past like hers usually left a person scarred for life.

Alfred sighed as she massaged all the kinks out of his neck and shoulder muscles. He knew Ash was scarred, but she was in much better shape than anyone else he knew who had been through what she had. Still, he regretted that she'd had such a painful past. He blamed himself although there was nothing he could have done to change things.

"Stop blaming yourself," Ash whispered in his ear.

"You always know what I'm thinking," he said on a chuckle.

Her hands dropped from his neck and she took the wingback chair beside him. "Because you and I are alike, Al. Austin is the changeling in the family."

Alfred's eyes met the icy grey stare of his sister. "I'm glad you're here, Ash," he said quietly.

She nodded solemnly, her auburn hair spilling over her shoulders like bloodstained cornsilk. "I am too. The Afterlife didn't agree with me." Her mobile lips curled in a smile that Alfred knew mocked her mortality. "I can't really call storms there. They have no weather, you know."

Ash's natural ability to control the elements had made her a prize among the Magia. That status had been both a bane and a boon. It had caused Alfred to have to bargain for her soul, something he would never tell her. Protecting Ash now was his overriding concern. He had to keep her safe until the Fire Storm occurred. Once the elemental phenomena of the Five Realms began, all he needed to do was send her to Antaeus International. After that, the forces of nature would take over.

He watched as his sister leaned over to grab the brandy decanter. The black halter top did nothing to hide the swirling lines stamped upon her skin. The tribal lines twisted along her spine from the small of her back up to the space between her shoulder blades, forming a stylized black dragon...with an emerald in its mouth.

To be continued...

Fire Storm, Tales of the Darkworld Book 7

About the Author

Lex has been writing stories and poems ever since she could hold a pencil. A few years ago, she got caught up writing in an online paranormal serial story. The story was very intense and a challenge to her writing skills. As she began to write more and more, fans of the story and her blog readers began to encourage her to submit her writing. Lex lives in Orange County, California with her long haired musician husband and her teen aged daughter. Lex loves loud music, reading hot stories, reading her friends' blogs and hanging out with them, enjoys building her own computers, and has a propensity for having very weird vivid dreams about Nikki Sixx.

Author Website – http://www.lexvalentine.com

Series Website: http://www.talesofthedarkworld.com

Author Newsletter - http://groups.yahoo.com/group/talesofthedarkworld

Author Blog – http://www.sunlightsucks.com

PPB

Pink Petal Books, an imprint of Jupiter Gardens Press, would like to invite you to explore the entire Jupiter Gardens, LLC family.

Don't forget to sign up for our reader's loop where we have monthly giveaways, chats, and more! Information can be found on the Pink Petal Books' website.

Jupiter Gardens, LLC – http://www.jupitergardens.com/

Pink Petal Books – http://www.pinkpetalbooks.com/

Jupiter Gardens Press – http://www.jupitergardenspress.com/

Thank you for buying and reading our books! Our authors appreciate your patronage.

If you enjoyed Fire Season, you might want to read the first two books in this series. The first chapters are provided here for your convenience.

Tales of the Dark World Book 1: Shifting Winds
by Lex Valentine
Chapter One

The huge vase of tulips hid the face of Granville Cemetery's receptionist as she carried the flowers into the elegant office of the Chief Financial Officer. At least they weren't red roses, Elysia thought as Marnie set the vase on the corner of the rosewood executive desk, pushing it closer to Elysia's morning cup of coffee.

"You'd think they'd be roses," the receptionist sniffed, unknowingly echoing her boss's thoughts. "You're the CFO here, Miss E. You deserve the best."

A choked chuckle emerged from one of two leather wingback chairs across the desk from Elysia. Marnie stepped closer to the occupied chair and swatted the tall blonde man on the back of the head.

"That's what *you* deserve, Mr. Colin. You're always in here bothering her. Don't you ever work?" she hissed at him sarcastically before walking out. The door shut softly behind her.

Instead of smirking at the way their receptionist goaded her younger brother, Elysia turned an evil look on Colin. "Don't say a word," she ground out, shifting her glare from her sibling to the card peeking from between a couple of purple tulip buds.

"Obviously, you know who they're from without opening the card," Colin observed.

"Yeah, I know who sent them." Elysia snatched up the card before Colin leaned over the desk and grabbed it. She stared at the expensive vellum, afraid to open the small envelope and have the sender confirmed.

"You're not going to tell me, are you?" Leather creaked as Colin sat forward in his chair. "C'mon, Lys. You always tell me your secrets. I never spill them to Marius."

Elysia winced at the mention of their older brother. The last thing she needed was for Marius to find out about the flowers. Not that Colin would tell. She always confided in him and he always kept it to himself. If not for Colin, she probably would have died of stress years ago. She had difficulty keeping her emotions bottled up inside her. This time, what bothered her was something Marius would want to know... and exploit.

And since it was something intensely personal, Elysia didn't want Marius to have even the tiniest inkling.

"Lock the door," she muttered grimly, turning the small cream-colored envelope over in her hands. She recognized the florist. They were the best in the county. "I can't have Marius walk in on this conversation."

Colin shot out of his chair with lightning fast reflexes that were a blur to human eyes. Fortunately, Elysia was no more human than Colin. In the blink of an eye, he returned to his chair, his mouth quirked in a grin that showed off the white points of his fangs. He must really be excited to hear her gossip if his fangs were out.

"So where were you last night?" he asked. "Is it related to the flowers?"

Elysia nodded. "I went to the Undertaker's Ball."

Colin's dark blue eyes widened. "You're shitting me. You really went to that thing?"

She sighed and ran a hand through her long honey blonde hair. "Yes. Marius bugged me about it for a solid week. I agreed to go just to get him off my back. I don't know why he couldn't have sent you. I'm sure you would have enjoyed it much more than me. You like dressing up on Halloween."

Colin laughed. "Of course, I do. I find it ironic to dress as Dracula or Nosferatu on Halloween. Last night, I did Nosferatu. I was scarier than Max Schreck, but that skull cap thing itched. And I had trouble getting the makeup off."

Elysia cocked an eyebrow up as her brother ruffled his dark blonde curls. She noticed tiny little bits of latex and glue in his hairline along with faint smudges of grey white makeup. "You've still got some on your face. Go upstairs and use that stuff Callie has in the prep room," she said. "That will take it off."

Colin nodded absently, his envious eyes on her coffee cup. "Yeah, I planned on it, but I had to stop here first to find out where you disappeared to last night. It's not like you to miss my Halloween party." He shook his head. "I can't believe you went to the Undertaker's Ball. For one, it's an industry thing. You don't like industry events. For another, I can't believe you caved in to Marius. You never do."

"I know. I know. Believe me; I hadn't intended to give in." Elysia sat back in her chair, placing her hands flat on the leather blotter on her desk. She stared at her long fingers for a moment, their plain unadorned expanse, short oval nails, uncolored, unexciting... except that last night they had been excited... in a frenzy of touching...

She jerked her mind away from those thoughts and looked up, meeting her brother's eyes. "Declan Antaeus was there." She said the words casually and watched her brother's eyes widen.

"Really?" Colin sat forward a little. "Did he talk to you about business? Marius said he's been angling for a meeting for six months."

"We didn't talk about work much," she mumbled, thinking they hadn't talked much at all.

"So what did you go as?"

Elysia rolled her eyes. "Elvira. I know, I know. Predictable and boring, but you should have seen Declan. He was worse."

Colin began to laugh. "Oh, no. He didn't. Tell me he didn't."

Elysia nodded. "He did. It was an obvious choice for a man of his height, but still, coming as the Grim Reaper was totally predictable and dull." She smiled at her brother as she recalled Declan stalking through the crowds dressed in the long black robe. "He was the only Reaper too."

Colin snorted derisively. "Of course. Everyone else had more creative costumes, didn't they?"

"Yes. He and I were probably the most boring costumes there, barring Alfred in a white sheet," she told him with a reminiscent smile.

"You're kidding. Alfred Stone wore a white sheet?" Colin's eyes danced with laughter at the thought of the head of the Funeral Director's Guild dressed as a ghost in a plain white sheet.

"He did. And he had that same shiny black suit on underneath. You know, the one you call his undertaker's suit."

The two of them laughed at the old-fashioned way of dressing that Alfred Stone of Stone Mortuary Services had cultivated. Alfred was a techie. He loved all things technology based, but when it came to clothes, he always looked like an undertaker from 1900. Elysia usually loved talking to Alfred because she was the computer geek at Granville Cemetery and they had a lot in common. However, she didn't like industry events. At least, not since she'd been rather spectacularly dumped by Alfred's brother Austin at the Darkworld's annual Funeral Director's convention three years ago. That experience taught her that the immortal world was just as hungry for gossip as the human world. Their hunger meant no one ever forgot the most humiliating and painful moment of her life.

Colin let out a sigh, his eyes meeting Elysia's. "So the tulips are from Declan Antaeus?"

"I think so." She opened the card that lay on her desk.

> *You are so much more beautiful than these flowers, but the texture of their petals reminded me of your skin. Dinner tonight? You and me and that gorgeous skin of yours...*
>
> *I'll call you.*
>
> *Declan*

Elysia sucked in a shaky breath. The man definitely had a way with words. Her heart pounded so hard that she wondered if Colin could hear it.

He stared at her with an arrested expression. "Holy shit, Lys. Don't tell me you slept with Declan Antaeus!" he said in a low, astonished voice.

Her lips tightened in annoyance. "Okay, I won't."

Colin flopped back in his chair, his expression concerned. "What possessed you to do such a thing?"

"Oh, I dunno, Colin. Hormones?" she quipped, her words just a touch angry. Her irritation grew. Colin acted as if she'd done something completely out of character. Declan Antaeus wasn't the first man she'd had a one night stand with, and he probably wouldn't be the last either. Although, as far as Colin knew, he was the first man she'd been with since Austin had dumped her three years before. Maybe that was what had Colin's briefs in a bunch. Luckily, the two other quick encounters she'd had in the last year hadn't been with anyone her brothers knew. "Declan is a good looking man," she admitted with a nonchalant shrug.

"He's a freaking shifter, Lys. A dragon. Not one of us." Colin's words were exasperated.

She gave him a sour look from her violet eyes. "I never realized what a prejudiced snob you are," she said stiffly, still wondering where her brother's weird attitude came from. She'd never noticed that he disliked dragons before.

Colin ran a hand through his hair, ruffling the golden curls. "I'm not! I swear I'm not. It's just that Marius has this fucked up notion that the reason Declan wants to meet with him is that Antaeus International intends to suck us up."

Elysia's eyes widened in surprise. Antaeus International was a huge conglomerate. They bought all of the little mom and pop mortuary and cemetery operations they could get their hands on. Afterward, they turned them all into highly profitable cremation based ventures. Granville Cemetery was very old and catered to the elite in the vampire world. They offered cremation, but vampires tended to not go that route. There was something about being reduced to a pile of ash that vamps didn't care for. They were influenced by too many cheesy movies about the undead, Elysia thought wryly.

"So Marius thinks AI is after us?" she asked aloud.

Colin nodded. "He said the only reason Declan would want a meeting is because AI wants to buy us out."

Her brother frowned ferociously. Obviously, Colin didn't favor the idea of being bought out. She didn't either, but unlike Colin, who rarely stuck his head into anything related to financials, she knew that the company's fiscal strength would withstand any buyout attempt by AI. However, she now wondered if Declan's plans for Granville Cemetery had fueled his easy acquiescence to her come on last night. She bit her lip.

Colin, seeing her expression and knowing her better than anyone, leaned forward and grabbed her hand. "I'm sure that's not why he slept with you, Lys," he said gently. "Every man in the Funeral Director's Guild, married or single or gay, wants to fuck you."

Elysia smiled. Colin exaggerated, but not by much unfortunately. It was one of the reasons Marius dealt with industry stuff instead of her, even though finance was her area. The fact that men didn't take her business acumen seriously had always been annoying in the past. For some reason, last night at the Undertaker's Ball, she just hadn't cared. She'd wanted to find someone who could take away the ache in her gut and Declan Antaeus fit the bill perfectly. Now, however, she had to figure out what to do about him. Obviously, he wanted to continue on from where they'd left off, but Elysia just wanted to forget it happened.

"It's hard to fake a hard on," she joked. "I'm pretty sure he wasn't thinking about mergers last night."

Colin let go of her hand and sat back, looking at the tulips. "Did you go to his place?"

Elysia made a face. "Yeah, after the first time."

Her brother's eyes registered shock. "Don't tell me you fucked him in the cemetery, Lys. That's just... just..."

"Too Halloween-ish even for you?" Elysia's expression turned wry.

"Well, yeah." Colin let out a deep sigh. "I know you don't listen to my advice very often, but Lys, have you thought about what you're getting into here? Declan Antaeus isn't the kind of guy you just have fun with."

"No worries, Colin. I'm not seeing him again."

Now, Colin gazed at her stupefied. "You're completely off your rocker, Elysia. You want a one nighter, but you pick up the man least likely to be interested in one? On top of that, the man is interested in buying us out. He's ruthless, dear sister, with a reputation for always getting what he wants. And you've now stepped right into his cross hairs. This is not going to go well."

Elysia bit back a sigh. She had a bad feeling that Colin was right. She glanced down at the card again and suppressed a shiver. She looked up into Colin's worried midnight blue eyes. She loved him to death, but she needed to think without the distraction of his questions and concerns. She pushed the vase of tulips toward him.

"Put that in the small visitation room," she ordered.

"That old vamp is in there. The one with no family." Colin's voice sounded puzzled.

"Exactly. No one sent any flowers. He pre-paid for his visitation and service and no one's come. Put the flowers in there. It won't look so sad then," she explained.

Her brother got up and picked up the vase. "You're making a big mistake with Declan Antaeus," he warned her as he strode to the door.

"You have no idea what I'm going to do, Colin."

Colin snorted in disgust. "Doesn't matter what you do. It's all a mistake. There is no winning with a man like him. Mark my words."

After Colin left, Elysia spun around in her chair, to gaze out the window at the expanse of green grass marked with upright tombstones. She didn't want to replay the night before, but after her conversation with Colin it was inevitable...

And the next book in the series...

Tales of the Darkworld Book 2: Hot Water

By Lex Valentine

Available Now from Pink Petal Books

Chapter One

Eden walked into Carpe Noctem wearing a short black dress and thigh high boots. The outfit, along with her long shaggy 'scene' haircut, made her seem nearly as young as the crowd that filled the trendy vampire themed nightclub. In truth, as an immortal, she looked younger than her actual years, appearing to be in her late twenties. Her tight, sexually provocative clothing had been chosen to aid the illusion of youth.

Trolling was tough business. Eden knew this from experience. With throngs of beautiful young things packing the clubs, finding someone to fuck could be a major undertaking if you didn't do something to set yourself above all the other immortals. Everyone wanted to get laid and available partners could be in short supply, especially when it came to vanilla sex. Despite what her older brother Sean thought, she figured her luck would hold better in the vampire bar than the ones she usually frequented. The cheesy vampire paraphernalia, the coffins, stakes and bats couldn't disguise the club's sophistication or fun factor. A sea of people, mostly humans dressed as vampires and true immortal Acerbian vampires, filled the club. Proving Sean wrong when he said the "Queen of Kink" would never go to Carpe Noctem, would give her immense satisfaction.

Ignoring the snarl that begged to get out whenever she thought of her elder brother, Eden turned toward the neon lit bar. She needed a drink before she contemplated the choice of partners offered by the club's patrons. As she elbowed herself a space at the end, her nose twitched. The scent of vanilla filled her senses, and her dragon suddenly itched to break free. Holy shit. Who the hell would walk into a social meat market smelling so innocent?

The smell came from her right. She wriggled in the tight quarters, trying to turn. Based on the sweet scent, she expected to see a woman. Instead, she found a tall man with midnight blue eyes smiling down at her.

"You just go right on trying to move," he quipped. "I'm enjoying it tremendously."

Eden's eyes narrowed. Every time she moved, her body rubbed up against his. Her hip dug into his groin and she could feel a slight telltale swelling there. Despite the fact that the man smelled all girly like a sugar cookie, the bulge held promise. She sniffed again. Sweet smelling. Smiling easily. No display of arrogance. A mellow and amused expression, eyes dancing with humor. Beta. He had to be. Her dragon stretched inside her, urging her to take him.

"Oh, really?" She raised one brow and wriggled against him again. The size of the ridge against her hip increased. Oh, yeah. He just might work out after all, she thought as she realized his more than adequate proportions weren't fully erect yet.

He nodded, his dark blue eyes gleaming as they raked over her from the top of her raven head to the tips of her designer boots. "Of course, we'd both enjoy it a lot more naked in my bed," he told her candidly.

Eden's pupils elongated as Blue Eyes roused her dragon. The scent of vanilla intensified.

"You don't believe in wasting time, I see." She turned, deliberately rubbing against him, breast to chest. In her boots, she almost matched his height.

He quirked a dark blond brow at her. "And you do? You can't tell me that the dragon in you isn't clawing to get at my cock."

Eden began to smile. He might not be a dragon, but he obviously knew them intimately. Good. One less thing she'd have to train him on. "You're a bold young thing, aren't you?"

He laughed. "I'm not as young as you think." His smile revealed vampire fangs.

She pondered the fangs for a moment. People often pretended to be vampires at Carpe Noctem. He could well be one of the wannabes. After all, she'd never met a vampire who smelt of vanilla before. Usually, the real ones smelled of blood. He didn't smell like a human either though. That vanilla scent masked his true nature and it annoyed her a little.

He shifted his hips against her and the hard ridge of his cock bumped against her belly. Her dragon poked her with its claws. Her thong grew damp as she rubbed against his erection. She finally decided he must be a real immortal, an Acerbian vampire.

"I just have a feeling I'm older than you. Indulge me," she said. "I like being a cougar." She reached down and boldly stroked the front of his jeans.

His engaging smile widened. "I'll be teacher's pet, I promise," he joked.

Her eyes narrowed. "Not a bad game. Have you been bad today? Do you need a spanking?"

As the words fell from her lips, she could have kicked herself. Tonight was supposed to be about vanilla sex, not toys or fetishes. However, the blond man just shrugged. "I'd rather just fuck you. All that other crap isn't necessary for me. As you can tell, I'm pretty much good to go."

His eyes gleamed preternaturally, answering her earlier questions about his status as an immortal. One hand cupped the side of her face, the long elegant fingers sliding into her dark hair. Angling his head toward hers, he dropped a quick kiss on her lips. An electric tingle went through Eden's body and her dragon came rushing to the surface of her skin.

When he deepened the kiss, parting her lips with his tongue, she sighed into his mouth. His free hand slid over her hip and curved over her taut buttock. She rubbed herself against him again as that sugar cookie scent grew stronger. Lifting her arms, she draped them over his broad shoulders, feeling the hard muscle and bone beneath his silk shirt. He sucked on her tongue and heat pooled deliciously between her thighs. Gods, he was hot!

"You know, at your ages, you should really get a room," a snarky voice spoke behind Eden.

The blond man lifted his head, his expression tinged with annoyance that only lasted a moment. Recognition bloomed in the midnight blue depths of his eyes and his lips twitched into a smile.

"Hey, I know you. You're..."

"Karl with a K... that elf with the internet gossip show... yeah, yeah," the elf said with a sarcastic laugh. "Everyone knows me, kid. Especially here."

Eden turned and looked at the man on the bar stool behind her. He had a half empty glass of Guinness in front of him and a bowl of bat-shaped pretzels. His grey-green eyes stared at her unblinkingly from behind wire-rimmed glasses. She frowned.

"You're immortal. Why are you wearing glasses?"

Karl gave her a look that would have withered most people. "I'm told wearing glasses gives you character. Since I don't have any character, I figured I'd manufacture some," he drawled.

Her blond hunk openly grinned now. Apparently, he found Karl's snarky sarcasm amusing. "I watch your show all the time. You have plenty of character. You're funnier than all the shows on TV."

"Tell that to my producer. He bitches daily that he's gonna fire me." Karl took a sip of his ale. "I meant what I said, you know. Get a room. All this grinding and humping is for the kids who got nowhere to go. You two are obviously old enough and wealthy enough to afford the room. So go there and grind. I don't like having to protect my drink from elbows that are in the throes of lust," he complained.

Mr. Sugar Cookie Scent chuckled. "Sure, Karl. Nice meeting you." He took hold of Eden's elbow.

Karl raised one brow at them. "We haven't been formally introduced, but I know who you are. And more importantly, I know who *you* are," he said, his eyes landing on Eden with a wicked gleam.

She opened her mouth to tell him to shut up when he waved a hand at her in a shooing motion. "I'm not telling. Names or lack of them is strictly between you two grinders. Now, would you mind letting me get back to my drinking here? Fucking horny immortals," he grumbled, turning away from them.

The blond man pulled her away from the bar toward the exit. "Where to?" he asked as they stepped out onto the street.

A cab whooshed up to the curb beside them and she opened the door, getting in. The blond man followed her. She gave the cabbie the name of a posh hotel on Park Avenue. As the cab took off, the blond man smiled. "From out of town? Me too."

Eden shrugged. "I'm here more than anywhere else. I travel almost constantly for work so I don't have a permanent place to live unless you count a dozen boxes of crap at my brother's house," she said in a dismissive tone.

"I can't imagine not having a home. I'm from the west coast myself."

Tall, blond, and vanilla's chatty behavior started to annoy her so she slid her hand up his jean-clad thigh and squeezed his half hard dick. It responded instantly to her touch. She smiled at him, her curved dragon fangs showing.

He sucked in a breath, his hand coming up to cup her breast. "I gather you're not much for chitchat," he said, his thumb teasing her nipple through the soft material of her dress.

"Nope," she replied. Naturally reticent, when her horny dragon raged, she was even less inclined to words. Only action of a sexual nature would calm the beast inside her. "Just looking for some vanilla sex. Nothing more. Nothing less."

"Well, just in case you feel the urge to shout my name later, it's Colin," he said and grabbed her by the back of the head.

Shock rippled through Eden as he held her firmly. He kissed her deeply, ravaging her mouth with the kind of kiss she'd expect from an Alpha, not a Beta like Colin. If his kiss hadn't completely overwhelmed her and made thinking next to impossible, she would have wondered if she had pegged him wrong. Where his kiss had been leisurely before, now it burned hot and urgent, demanding a response from her rather than accepting what she doled out to him.

Abruptly, he let her go. Her chest heaved as she sucked in great gulps of air. Colin's eyes glinted enigmatically at her in the dim light of the cab. "You gotta be more careful about judging a book by its cover," he growled.

She blinked. He looked at her with a feral light in his eyes. Ho-ly shit. She'd never misjudged an Alpha before. Of course, her familiarity with vampires fell far below that of dragons and fae men. She'd always been rather skittish around vamps. All that biting and blood sucking...

Colin took her chin in his hand, forcing her to meet his gaze. The midnight blue irises glowed preternaturally again, and she could feel the steely strength in his long elegant fingers. "You're lucky I'm a nice guy and all I want is to fuck your pretty pink pussy," he whispered. "Walking into a vampire club and making snap judgments about my kind can get you drained, despite the fact that you're a dragon."

Her eyes widened a little. He smiled then, and the sunny, amusing persona he'd displayed at the club, the persona that had shouted Beta to her, snapped back into place. "You are going to let me fuck your pretty pink pussy, aren't you?" he asked as his fingers turned from steel to silk, sliding warmly across her skin.

Eden nodded. Several strands of her raven hair caught in the golden stubble that covered his jaw. His vanilla, sugar cookie scent grew stronger and she realized his arousal intensified it. The more aroused he became, the stronger the scent grew. The sweet smell flooded her entire being, making her mouth water. She wondered what he tasted like...

In a split second, the dragon within her roared to life. She pushed Colin against the back of the cab's seat and kissed him hard, her lips and tongue sucking urgently at his. The heat and depth of the kiss pushed her arousal up several notches. It had been a long time since a man had affected her so strongly, and never had one's scent overpowered her as Colin's did. Potent and distinctive, she would have been able to find him in a crowd of thousands at Madison Square Garden. Definitely something to remember if she ever had to hunt for him.

Colin's hands slid up under the hem of her mini dress, his fingers digging into her ass. She rubbed herself against him and he rewarded her with another growl. Pure sex emanated from the sound, with none of the male fierceness that had colored it previously. The sound skittered along her nerve endings, reaching her inner dragon and rousing the beast's tremendous sexual appetite.

Heat and wetness rushed to the sensitive flesh between her thighs. Colin's nostrils flared and she knew he had caught the scent of her sex. Beneath her hand, his cock had swollen to a satisfying proportion. The long thick ridge behind the zipper of his jeans promised to fill her as no one had before. Size had never mattered to her, but then, she'd never had someone as big as Colin promised to be.

The cab screeched to a stop, the centrifugal force pushing her back against the seat and away from the press of Colin's body. She sprawled awkwardly; her skirt hitched up so far her thong showed. The driver didn't even bother to look in the rear view mirror at her. Colin ran his hands over his face, then opened the door and got out. He reached in, holding out a hand for her. She put hers in it and let him pull her out of the cab. Tugging her dress down, she waited as he paid the driver.

When Colin turned toward her, she saw the feverish glitter in his eyes. He apparently didn't care that anyone who chose to look at his crotch would see the bulge of his erection. He took her arm and they walked boldly into the lobby of the expensive hotel. Exhilaration swept through Eden as they headed toward the elevator. Once in the car, she pushed the six and the car swept upward. Her dragon clawed at her insides. She was so aroused, she expected her cream to drip down her bare thighs any moment.

At her floor, they got off the elevator, and she turned down the plushly carpeted corridor, her long legs eating up the distance to her room. As she neared it, she took out her keycard. She stopped in front of 669, slipping the keycard in the slot. Colin chuckled at the room number. Moments later, he closed the door, sticking the Do Not Disturb sign on it. When he turned toward her, she reached back and unzipped her dress, letting it fall to the floor.

Standing in front of Colin in her black silk thong and leather boots, a sense of empowerment filled her. Her fingers twitched, aching for the thick handle of her whip. Colin looked at her hand and arched one blond brow in amusement, almost as if he could read her thoughts. He casually pulled off his jacket and tossed it on the chair, following it with his shirt.

Eden's eyes raked over the muscles of his arms and chest. He had a fine boned aristocratic caste to his build, with pale gold skin, a shade or two lighter than her own tan. The muscles of his arms, pecs, and shoulders were sculpted and well defined, but not bulky. His rock hard abs had classic six pack ridges. A fine dust of blond hair encircled each of his pale brown nipples... pale brown pierced nipples.

Her lips quirked in a smile. He really wasn't what he appeared to be, she thought as he bent and removed his shoes and socks. When he straightened, she briefly eyed his long narrow feet. Elegant like his hands. Her gaze shifted to those hands. They pulled down the zipper of his jeans, pushing the denim down his muscular thighs. He kicked the jeans away and hooked his thumbs in the waistband of his boxers. She stared at him thoughtfully, deciding that he had predictable taste in underwear. He seemed like a boxers kind of guy. With a practiced flick, the garment in question hit the floor and he kicked them in the same direction as the jeans.

"Will I do?" he asked, as her eyes wandered his hard body. Dark gold hair arrowed from his navel to his groin. She saw that he kept himself well trimmed and thought that it extended to his balls too. Even from a distance, they seemed smooth. He had a larger cock than the bulge in his jeans had given away, she noted, taking in his girth and length. Her mouth watered at the thought of licking him.

"I believe you will." Desire turned her voice husky and unconsciously, her fingers reached down to her panty line to stroke over her clan mark. The dragon inside her began to pace. Touching the swirling lines of the clan mark that covered the soft skin inside her hipbone made her even hornier.

"Your clan mark?" he asked quietly, watching her stroke it.

She nodded and he walked toward her, reaching out to brush one long finger over the mark. Her inner dragon preened at his touch. She knew the mark just looked like a tribal dragon tattoo to the uninitiated. However, Colin seemed to know about clan marks and how they reacted to touch.

"You're a black dragon. I'm not sure I recognize the clan though," he murmured, circling her and looking up and down her body.

"It doesn't matter. All you really want is to fuck my pretty pink pussy, right?" she reminded him with a lift of her brows.

Colin smiled angelically. "For now, yes, although, you have yet to show it to me..."

As his voice trailed away, Eden bent over and unzipped her boots. She could feel Colin's eyes on her breasts as if he touched her. The weight of his gaze made her rush and she kicked the expensive designer footwear off, something she never did. She lifted her head, her eyes holding his as she shimmied out of the black silk thong.

Inside her, the dragon roared, knowing that the tension they shared would soon be released. Eden walked over to the bed and ripped the covers back. Lying on the sheets, she spread her legs so that Colin could see the pussy he'd promised to fuck. She didn't need a mirror to know that her flesh glistened wetly in the low light. She could feel her swollen, sensitive lips throbbing. She stroked her hand over the clan mark and her nipples tightened painfully.

If you want it, come and get it, bite boy. Standing there staring at it, doesn't do either of us any good.

Colin's eyes jerked to hers and for a split second she had the weird sense that he had heard her thoughts, something that sent fear arcing through her. But then he flashed a seductive smile that widened as he started toward her. In a flood of lust that drowned her momentary fear, she gazed mesmerized at the thick erection that bobbed with each of his steps.

"It really is very pink and very pretty," he said softly, his tone filled with satisfaction.

When he reached the side of the bed, his long fingers trailed over her knee and up the inside of her thigh. Her heart thundered in her chest and her dragon's harsh breathing sent a trail of smoke from her nostrils.

Colin leaned over her, his hands denting the mattress on either side of her hips as he sat on the edge of the bed. "How much foreplay do you want, baby? Because as far as I'm concerned, what happened in the cab was all I need."

Eden licked her lips, watching as Colin's eyes darkened even more. "I don't need any more teasing. Just fuck me hard and fast before I explode from looking at you."

She didn't know what to expect, but what happened next still surprised her. With an economy of movement that made it all seem like a single smooth move, Colin reached out, flipped her onto her belly, pulled her hips back against his and thrust the entire length of his cock into her throbbing wetness. She let out a startled half yelp, half moan. He filled her so tightly it bordered on pain. Taking someone as big as him without any warning had driven every ounce of air from her lungs.

Colin's fingers roughly pinched and twisted her hard nipples. Pleasure ripped through her in a great wave. She had no idea how he knew what she liked. He certainly didn't look like a rough sex sorta guy. He looked cultured and refined, the elegant and arrogant sort who liked to order women to service him.

He jerked her up off her hands, his chest cradling and supporting her torso. His hips stilled as his hands swept over her body, finding all the places she most liked to be touched. When she moaned uncontrollably, he licked her neck and she shivered. The most incredible sensations buffeted her body when his tongue stroked over her skin. She almost asked him to bite her, but he bent her over again. Her palms hit the mattress as his hips slammed into her ass. He pulled back and thrust into her forcefully.

Eden's pussy stretched to accommodate him while clinging to his thickness. He fucked her harder than she'd ever been fucked before. The head of his cock battered her G-spot with every thrust. Shivers of pleasure racked her body. Her orgasm crested and she cried out, tossing her head.

Colin chuckled but his tempo didn't lessen. He gave her exactly what she'd asked for. She shuddered and gasped for air, her heart racing thunderously. Unbelievably, as one long finger flicked over her clit, she found herself coming again.

She knew he could feel her spasms, feel her pussy clamping down on his thick cock. His strokes became shorter. The slap of his hips against her ass grew more frantic. His teeth nipped the back of her neck as his hands tightened on her thighs.

"Oh, baby. Come for me one more time. You can do it," he growled.

His tongue licked at her neck in time to the glide of his fingers against her clit. His cock filled her so full he could barely press inside her despite the fact that she was wetter than she had ever been. His thumb stroked over her mark and inside her, the dragon roared as heat flooded her veins. Her pussy clutched his cock as her whole body vibrated in a third orgasm.

With a muffled cry, Colin came. His cock jerked inside her and she could feel the gush of hot seed that filled her. Shaking uncontrollably, her arms gave out and her face landed on the sheet, her ass still in the air as Colin's cock throbbed inside her, spurts of cum still erupting from him. Finally, he pulled out of her. She moaned at the feel of his flesh separating from hers, leaving her sensitive, open and exposed.

Colin flopped onto his back beside her and her knees gave out, her lower body sprawling bonelessly on the bed. They looked at each other, both of them gasping for air. Then Colin reached out and brushed a lock of hair off her face.

"I'll give you fifteen minutes to recover. Then I'm pounding that pretty pink pussy again after I lick it into submission."

Eden's eyes popped open in astonishment. She didn't know what astonished her more, the fact that he would be ready again so soon or the way he took control. His lips curved in a grin.

"I don't think you'll need any of the toys I'm sure you have here. We'll just fuck. I'm good at it and I like to do it for hours." His midnight blue eyes twinkled at her. "Unless you're sending me away now that you've come."

Although he hadn't framed his words as a question, she shook her head anyway. "I don't think I can send you away. At least, not until I'm worn out and can't walk," she replied, her own smile growing as approval flashed across his face.

"Good." He leaned over and kissed her hard. "Time for tongues and fingers to discover cocks and pussies."

He grabbed her hand and placed it on his half-hard cock, still wet with her juice and his seed. She stroked him, wondering why she'd never been into biters before. Unbidden, her mind went back the phone call that had sent her storming into Carpe Noctem looking to get laid. An outcast to her family, she rarely went home, rarely participated in family events. Even so, she loved her siblings. When one of them had accused her of being the Queen of Kink, an unfeeling bitch of a slut who lived to get off, it stung. Those words from someone she had looked up to her entire life, struck deeply into emotions she struggled daily to control. To survive the pain, she'd retreated into the cold bitch persona she'd been accused of.

Now, that same self-preservation kept the lid on her emotions, when she looked at Colin. The core of her wanted to know him, but the icy bitch who'd taken control of her during that painful phone call refused to let go. The bitch coolly surveyed Colin, wondering why she hadn't hit on vampires before. She snarkily thought that if she had known biters were this good, she would have been picking them up regularly from Carpe Noctem. And that same cold bitch decided that she had more one item she could add to her sexual buffet menu now that she knew about vampires' stamina.

Inside her, behind the icy bitch, the real Eden gazed at Colin's beautiful face and wished her life was different.

Enjoy the first chapter from...
Love is Scary by Cheryl Dragon
Chapter One

Starting a new business was one of the scariest things a person could do in any economy. But for Ryan Elliott, the hot guy helping him gets things off the ground was even scarier. Ryan had been emailing and trading phone calls with Wes Taylor for months in the hope that this venture would materialize. One of Wes' creations, a haunted house in New Orleans, had blown Ryan away in California, so Ryan had tracked the man down. He'd never seen a picture of Wes and never imagined the creative genius would turn out to be so unassumingly sexy.

In the building Ryan had recently bought on the cheap, thanks to the crippling real estate bust, he tried not to stare at Wes' hard body encased in worn dark blue jeans and a T-shirt about Cajuns. Wes was from New Orleans and had traveled here for this job. He'd leave Vegas once the haunted house was up and running. Ryan had to remember this visit was temporary. But the hard muscles on Wes's six-foot-four-inch frame made Ryan forget everything. Wes's green eyes caught Ryan's and the sizzle hit him.

Clutching his travel mug, Ryan sipped his coffee despite the heat of a Vegas summer and the sparks with Wes. Caffeine and work were his addictions. Men he could avoid—most of the time.

"Look okay?" Ryan gestured to the big empty club area.

Wes turned to him and smiled. "Looks great. You've got room for the bar in back and plenty to work with in the front club section. The place looks laid out already."

"It was a bar before with a huge dance club in front. The former owner couldn't handle the mortgage anymore so it was a steal. Needs a little work." Ryan looked around the unfinished space and tried not to stare at Wes. Wearing black dress pants and gray striped shirt for a meeting that afternoon, Ryan felt overdressed. Juggling his day job in advertising and a new small business venture sounded crazy, even to him. His family back home thought he was nuts. *Keep your day job and stay safe*. They all wanted security but then again, so did everyone else.

Ryan needed to try. His idea was solid, if he could make it happen. Wes had the experience.

"We'll add on a little in front, make it more of a maze feel. Go through several rooms and themes and the end will dump them into the bar area." Wes nodded.

"You have people who can do this?" Ryan asked.

"I brought the key members of my team. Don't worry." Wes patted Ryan's shoulder. "Your idea is great. An adults only haunted house with a bar and club at the end."

"Horror movies are huge hits year round now. Why not have a year round attraction in Vegas?" Ryan smiled. Wes' approval meant a lot. He'd been in the haunted house business for years. His designs were elaborate and innovative.

"The *adults only* part might help or hurt. I haven't decided yet." Wes measured the front door, leaning over to read the tape.

Ryan tried not to look at Wes's tight jean-covered ass. "Well, its Vegas. T&A sells. Plus, if you look at all the DVD sales of horror movies, it's the unrated versions that do the best. Producers film stuff they know will get cut for the theaters just to put it in the unrated DVDs. If this takes off, we can always do a PG version for kids. No bar, but food and stuff. That'd be phase two. One step at a time."

"Sounds good to me. I appreciate the work and the confidence."

"I've seen your work. It's excellent. New Orleans still slow?" Ryan asked.

Wes nodded. "Not everyone moved back. A lot of crime and poverty still. Nothing like the tourism we used to have. I travel around to do haunted houses so this is nothing new. But I used to do my own unique one in New Orleans every year. However, the last few years, it hasn't paid off."

"That's too bad. It's pretty down there." Ryan took another drink of coffee. "I definitely want to update the theme here every year. So I'll be calling you back in if that works."

"First let's get you opened. I'm not qualified to set up the bar but I'll get the building permits, a small construction crew together and start work soon."

The control freak in Ryan took over. "You'll show me the plans before you start anything major. I want to be involved even if my schedule doesn't really let me."

Wes moved in closer and, to Ryan, made the huge club feel like a tiny closet.

"Don't worry, I'll keep you advised. I'll have sketches done tonight. I'm a night owl and do my best creative work after dark. We could meet in the morning to go over them if that works." Wes looked him in the eye.

"I can't tomorrow. I have a meeting in the morning and conference calls in the afternoon. I can swing the club but I'd like to keep the steady cash flow of my day job. I might be leaning on you more than your other clients." Ryan hoped that he didn't sound as sexual as his mind played it.

"No worries, Ryan. I don't blame you. A constant income to fall back on makes it easier to go after your dreams. I'm behind you." Wes stood only inches away.

The sexy smell of wood and leather came from Wes. It had to be a tool belt. Ryan wanted to lean in and get more, but he'd always kept his private life out of business. It made things so much easier in the Vegas advertising world that revolved around sex. He spent so much time working that it left him with no social life. "Thanks. My family thinks this is all crazy. They think I should just keep my job and forget about the club."

"You want a tip?" Wes leaned in.

Ryan nodded and locked his eyes on Wes's mysterious green ones.

"Don't listen to them. Play it safe your whole life and you'll end up wondering what if. I did some construction, got roped into doing play sets and then haunted houses. I finally found something I loved. Scaring people, the designs and mechanisms. It's a thrill for me. I could have had a safe boring construction job and now I'd be totally out of work with building so slow. In New Orleans, it's not moving as fast as people thought it would to recover. But I can do this, turn a club into a haunted house. So you're sticking with the theme we discussed?"

Ryan cleared his throat. "For the opening, yes. Gaming hell. Haunted Vegas casino. Roulette wheels, slot machines, naughty show girls, etc."

Wes made notes on a pad and shoved it into his belt and the short pencil behind his ear. "Got it. Sounds good. I've got some of the concepts and sketches done. I'll flesh it out now that I've seen the space. It'll give me something to do this afternoon."

"You're settled in the hotel room?" Ryan had called in a favor and got Wes and his core team some comped rooms at a hotel on the strip.

"Yes, it's great. I never had a room like that in Vegas before. Why don't you come by after your afternoon meeting? We could go over the concept and grab dinner."

Ryan swallowed hard. He wanted to be alone in a hotel room with Wes, badly. They'd hit it off over the phone, email, and texts. But in person, the chemistry was hard to fight. "I may have to take the clients to dinner. Could be late."

"I understand. Gotta keep your bosses happy. Call my cell when you're done. I'll be up, if you're up for it. Got my number?"

He had it memorized, but Ryan tried to play it cool. "Yeah, it's programmed into my contacts. Sounds good. I'll call." Definitely want to keep the focus on the business. He checked his watch. No way could he be late.

"One last question and I'll let you go." Wes took a step back. "I assume since you said T&A, it's a straight adult concept?"

Ryan felt his skin go hot. Wes made him. "Yes, straight. We need to play to the odds in Vegas. Is that a problem?" His instinct told Ryan that Wes was gay.

"No problem here. Naked ladies make money and it's better. They don't distract me from my work." He kicked a broken floor tile with his alligator skin boot. "See you tonight."

Ryan smiled and lifted his mug. He didn't trust his voice just then. He watched Wes walk out to his rented truck.

Ryan knew he was in trouble.

~* * *~

Setting his sketches out on the coffee table, Wes checked the logic in his flow and it worked. His creativity took over and went all out. The vision and scope came together well.

Wes sat back on the sofa and took a deep breath. It felt great to be on a design project instead of demolishing an abandoned, or condemned, home. The creative work had dried up in the Big Easy and even building was slow.

Ryan's image crept back into his mind. Wes tried to ignore the stab of arousal. Long distance, their business plans matched up perfectly. They were on the same page and it all clicked. He should've known that'd spell trouble.

No way would Wes screw up this job by hitting on Ryan, no matter how hard Ryan stared. The chemistry was hard to ignore. Besides, Wes had sworn off relationships. Ryan didn't seem like the random, or casual, sex type.

Wes's cell phone rang a Vegas tune and he grabbed it. At some point, he'd given Ryan his own ring tone and Wes felt like an idiot with a crush. "Wes Taylor," he answered like any other business call.

"It's Ryan. Too late to look at your samples?" he asked.

Wes almost said no just to keep his self-control. But business had to come first. "Never too late for me. Come over whenever you want."

"Okay, I'll be there in ten minutes. Can I get you a coffee?" he offered.

"Nope, I'm good. See you soon." Wes ended the call. Vegas prices were crazy. Wes had made a run to a discount store and stocked up on water, soda, beer, and snacks.

Wes straightened up the hotel room a little and grabbed himself a bottle of water. Ryan knocked on the door and Wes' stomach knotted. This high-strung ad exec with a dream somehow had gotten to Wes.

He opened the door and Ryan smiled, sexy as ever. Those hazel eyes fit Ryan perfectly, a mix of things in which someone could get lost. "Come in," Wes said.

Ryan entered, still toting his travel mug of coffee. Wes noted that Ryan's light brown hair was a bit more mussed than earlier and his sleeves were rolled to the elbow. Just what Wes needed to see, lean muscled arms. "I've got water, beer, and soda." Ryan had to be overdosing on the coffee now, since it was now after eleven.

"I'm good." Ryan sat on the sofa and looked at the sketches.

"Did you go to some fancy steakhouse for dinner with the clients?" Wes asked.

"Yeah, at the hotel the clients are staying. I didn't really eat much. These sketches are perfect."

Wes sat down next to Ryan. "Glad you like them. I've got some leftover chicken strips in the little fridge if you want. They're spicy."

Ryan scooted back a few inches. "No thanks. I don't eat much in general. Coffee and work."

"You'd never make it in New Orleans. Food and fun is our business."

"I like New Orleans, just not a big eater. Vegas has a ton of food but I live here. I don't even notice it anymore." He grabbed one of the sketches. "She's topless?"

Wes chuckled. "Yeah, a topless zombie blackjack dealer. I don't draw breasts a lot. The players are transfixed on her assets and when people get closer to look, the players turn on them and they're disfigured. They try to pull the people in to take their places."

"Perfect." Ryan leaned closer.

"And there are more people who jump out from behind and guide them to the roulette wheel." Wes inhaled Ryan's subtle aftershave and the scent of coffee. Fighting this attraction would really be impossible.

"What happens at the roulette wheel?" Ryan looked up at him.

Wes' brain stopped over-thinking things.

"People keep their hands on their bet and all the losers get their hands chopped off. You'll like the craps table. A hot naked guy lying on his stomach is the table. His back's painted and they throw dice on it."

Ryan stiffened. "Why would I like that? It's good to have something for the women to enjoy as well. It needs to be balanced, but why would I care?"

Grabbing Ryan by the shoulders, Wes suppressed a chuckle. A closet case. At least there was no pressure. "Don't worry. I'm not after a relationship. I've been screwed too many times. But you're driving me crazy." Wes yanked Ryan's dress shirt open and pushed him back on the couch.

Ryan held onto Wes' shoulders. "What are you doing?" he asked.

If that was his idea of fighting off a man, Wes knew he'd win in seconds. Stretching out on Ryan's lean form, Wes cupped the back of Ryan's head and pulled him closer. Wes kissed him, no finesse or subtly. He possessed Ryan's mouth.

Ryan's hands pulled on Wes' t-shirt as his mouth opened eagerly. Just sex! Wes reminded himself as the warmth of Ryan's hard body melted what resolve he had left. This was no club hook up.

Kissing down Ryan's lean chest, Wes could feel every muscle with his tongue as he teased Ryan's nipples and let the crisp chest hair graze his cheek. He unbuckled Ryan's belt and opened his fly over the hard cock. His boxers tented and Wes teased him through the slippery fabric.

"Don't." Ryan's hips lifted in direct opposition to his words.

Not interested in high school games, Wes let go of Ryan and sat up. "Okay."

Ryan's eyes opened wide and his ragged breath slowed. "What the hell?"

"I'm tired of games. I've been through enough crap. I don't want a relationship. I've tried it and always get the wrong guy. But I'm not going to play sex games either. You want me or you don't. Don't be a tease."

"You're serious. Just sex?" Ryan asked.

"Yeah, nothing more. Business and sex. I can't deny the attraction but I'm done getting the short end in a relationship. I'm tired of trying. But I'm not into games like *hard to get* either." Wes sat back on the sofa and took a deep breath. "Let's get back to work. Just forget the sex."

He meant it, but when Wes felt a tug on his denim fly, he knew Ryan had reconsidered the situation. Pulling off his shirt, Wes watched as his erection sprang free into Ryan's large hands.

Ryan sucked Wes' balls not saying a word. Wes groaned, lifting his hips. He grabbed the back of Ryan's neck and guided him up to the shaft. Ryan's tongue snaked around and up, leaving Wes off balance and in need.

"Suck it!" Wes couldn't decide if Ryan was a tease or less experienced than he thought. But Ryan made his way up the long member to the tip and finally sucked. Thrusting up, Wes kept a hand on Ryan's neck, pressing him down to suck further.

Ryan's tongue teased the tip of Wes' cock but his strong lips pressed to the flesh about halfway down his cock. His hand gripped the bottom half of his erection and squeezed until Wes' hips fucked up in time.

Cursing, Wes thrust harder when Ryan pulled his mouth away. His tongue flicked over the tip and Wes moaned. "Ryan, you're a damn tease."

Ryan's probing tongue worked the tip until Wes thought he'd come. Then Ryan sucked down to the base. Finally, Ryan hit a pattern of sucking and release that made Wes grab the back of the sofa and fight his release to keep the contact going.

Ryan's persistent tongue rubbed the head of Wes' cock until he gave in and came on Ryan's broad tongue. With a whole day of thinking about Ryan, Wes had no chance to last long.

Wes watched Ryan suck and swallow every drop and then lick the shaft from base to tip. Just when Wes thought it was his turn, Ryan shifted focus to Wes' sac and rolled it around in his mouth and tugged.

Playtime had to wait. Wes needed to suck Ryan off. He grabbed the sexy man by his expensive collar and pulled him up until they were face-to-face.

"Sorry, I grew up in the bible belt. I tried to not...I don't have a lot of experience. I can't stop." Ryan exhaled hard.

Wes smiled. "Stop fighting it." He kissed Ryan slowly and slid them both off the couch and onto the floor. Pushing the coffee table out of the way, he pressed Ryan flat on his back and kept kissing him.

Reaching into those fancy boxers, Wes freed Ryan's cock and rolled his balls firmly in his hands.

"Wes, please." Ryan changed the angle of the kiss and wrapped his arms around Wes' neck.

They both needed this. Wes could feel Ryan's cock pulsing. Moving lower, he kissed Ryan's neck and slipped his grip to kiss Ryan's hard chest. This time he moved swiftly down to Ryan's stomach and hips.

"Yes!" Ryan gripped Wes' hair and pushed him down to his cock.

Wes tongued Ryan's sac, teasing as good as he'd gotten. Sucking Ryan's balls and rubbing a finger beneath them, Wes watched Ryan's body bow.

"I can't take it," Ryan insisted.

"But you can dish it out?" Wes took pity on him and sucked Ryan's cock into his mouth fully. The head bumped the back of his throat and Wes groaned with the intense satisfaction of pushing his own limits. Ryan was the perfect size. He could deep throat him and get enough pressure to turn Wes on as well.

Thrusting up carefully, Ryan paused. "I don't want to hurt you."

Wes groaned and released Ryan's cock. "Not possible. I have plenty of experience." He licked his fingers and slid them between Ryan's firm ass cheeks to rub the sensitive spot between Ryan's sac and asshole.

"Oh, God!" Ryan's eyes rolled back in his head.

"Exactly. Fuck my mouth and don't play games." Wes nipped at Ryan's balls before sucking his erection to the base again. He rubbed and pinched Ryan's rear until Ryan pumped up, fucking Wes' mouth like a desperate man.

Pressing his fingers firmly against the length of Ryan's shaft with each cock thrust, Wes knew Ryan wouldn't last long. Ryan gripped Wes' hair and fucked faster. Wes increased the suction, trying to keep Ryan's cock. Suddenly Ryan pressed and held, coming deep.

Wes' mouth was full and he let the taste of Ryan roll over his tongue as Ryan thrust a few final times. "That was incredible." Ryan tried to sit up.

Holding the sexy man down, Wes licked and sucked Ryan's tired cock before rubbing his tongue over the tip for the final drops.

"Yeah." Wes knew amazing sex when he had it, but he had to stick to the plan. He couldn't let himself get romantic about Ryan. "We better get back to work. The crew will be there at eight am sharp." He wanted to kiss Ryan and get things going again so Wes could fuck that tight ass, but not now. He needed to remain in control or he'd really be screwed.

Made in the USA